Literary Chaos

Michael Landon Jr.

& Cindy Kelley

Copyright © 2025

All Rights Reserved

Dedication

For our grandchildren.

You can have a thousand adventures with a book in your hand.

Dear Reader:

Stories are not confined to a single genre; they span various categories, from science fiction to historical fiction, adventure to romance, mystery to fantasy. This vast range ensures that there is a story for every taste, allowing you to explore different worlds and discover what resonates with you the most.

The story that you're about to embark on is an amalgam of all the genres, hence the title, *Literary Chaos*. And inside these pages, we have hidden some delightful Easter eggs, featuring hidden quotes and names from some of the greatest classics of all time. It's a fun challenge to see if you can identify them as you read along. It adds an extra layer of enjoyment and appreciation for these works. So, keep your eyes peeled for those hidden gems.

In conclusion, my dear Bookworm, reading the classics is like discovering a treasure trove of wisdom, imagination, and adventure. They have stood the test of time and continue to captivate generations of readers. So, I urge you to delve into this world of literary wonders and let your imagination soar.

Happy reading … and hunting, and may the classics guide you on extraordinary journeys!

Warmest regards,

Michael Landon Jr. & Cindy Kelley

Contents

Chapter 1
We're All Damaged, Somehow

The faded gray Victorian house was the neighborhood eyesore. While the other historical homes in the Boston suburb had been lovingly cared for, the three-story place on the corner had been long neglected. There were overgrown bushes on either side of the steps leading to a front porch littered with autumn leaves. The once-white picket fence around the yard had become a weathered, nondescript color, with several of the pickets missing or lying on the ground. Even the engraved brass plate next to the front door that read "built-in 1918" was crooked and hanging by one nail.

From the street, the place looked deserted until a girl appeared in a second-story window. She stood there for a moment, seeming to study the world outside the dirty glass, and then disappeared.

Joanna "Jo" March stepped away from her bedroom window and plopped down on her bed to open her Chromebook. While the song "Some Things Are Meant to Be" from the Broadway show *Little Women* played loudly on a small Bluetooth speaker, Jo studied the supply list her new school had emailed. She needed some of the usual stuff: spiral notebooks and pencils, a calculator (which she considered ridiculous since she had a calculator on her phone), a protractor, and a box of Sharpies. Her mom had asked about textbooks, but the school told her all books were online. Jo needed her laptop, but she would miss having actual books to study from, like at her old school.

Being the new kid was not how she'd envisioned her eighth-grade year. The thought made her queasy, but she pushed it aside and surveyed the room she'd moved into just five days before. There were still several boxes yet to be unpacked, but they were things she didn't need. In fact, she was tempted never to open them and to tell her mom to donate everything to the local charity. It sounded like a good plan until she worried that maybe they had packed one or two of her books in the wrong boxes. She couldn't imagine parting with any of her books, and her extensive collection was a hodgepodge of every genre imaginable. *Into the Wild, It, The Velveteen Rabbit, The Diary of a Young Girl, The Bone Clocks, The Wonderful Wizard of Oz,* and many more had already been carefully placed on the shelves around the room.

Jo plucked a small wire cage from her bureau and surveyed the space, her eyes peeled. She spotted a tiny brown mouse wearing a green vest cruising quickly across the tops of the shelved books.

"Come on, Nimble. I don't want to be late for my first day. It's really gonna suck being the new kid!"

Nimble continued to jump from book to book. "Stop right now, or I'm leaving you behind in this creepy old house."

Nimble stopped, and Jo chuckled at the title of the book, *The Life and Perambulation of a Mouse.* "Very clever, smarty mouse." Jo held out her hand, and Nimble stepped into her palm. Jo picked up her iPhone and cut the music off. Almost instantly, a vent on her floor carried the angry voices of her parents.

"I still don't understand what in the world possessed you to bid on a foreclosure without telling me!" her mom said.

Her dad answered, "We've been over this a hundred times. We were both stressed about our landlord doubling our rent, and we needed to find a solution."

"And you didn't think to ask your wife, who is a *realtor*, for crying out loud, what I thought about it?" Her mom's voice was getting louder.

Jo didn't wait to hear her dad's response. She stepped away from the vent and carefully placed Nimble into a small "traveling" cage. She held it up so they were almost nose to nose.

"Not a peep out of you, and we'll be fine, Nimble. Hear me? Not a peep!"

The mouse regarded her for a moment, then turned and settled into the corner of his cage. Jo tucked him into her backpack beside her laptop and hurried out of her room.

As she entered the kitchen, her parents were squared off in the middle of the room. A coffee cup dangled from her dad's fingers, and her mom pointed at him with a spatula. As soon as they saw Jo, they both relaxed and smiled at her.

"Good morning," Jo said.

"Morning, Munchkin," her dad said.

Jo hurried across the kitchen floor and put her backpack on the counter.

"Whoa, slow your roll, Jo. Nobody has time for a fall this morning," her mom said.

"I haven't had stitches in a month," Jo countered. "I'm good."

"Let's try for a record two months without a trip to the ER," her mom said. "Besides, I don't even know where the closest hospital is on this side of Boston."

"Ready for your first day of school?" her dad asked.

"Sure. Ready," she answered. "How's the manuscript coming along, Dad? Last night, when I kissed you goodnight, your protagonist had just discovered Hitler's secret hiding place."

"I re-read that chapter this morning, and I'm pleased to report I'm not scrapping it and starting over." Her dad shot a look at her mom before smiling at Jo. "Thanks for asking."

"Let's see if you can get really focused on figuring out this mess you've saddled us with," her mom said with a failed attempt at a playful tone.

"I, too, wonder why progress looks so much like destruction," he said.

"Progress? There was no hot water again this morning, so I had to take a cold shower."

"Cold showers are actually good for you, Mom. They bolster your immunity against the common cold and improve your circulation."

Her mom glanced over at her dad, who shifted his weight nervously.

"She's right, Eve. In fact, cold showers are even supposed to combat symptoms of depression," he said.

"The only thing I'm depressed about is this house, Adam," Evelyn said. And then, as if on cue, she sneezed.

"Bless you," Adam and Jo said at the same time. Adam sighed. "Listen, if you could only try to see the potential in this place …"

"You said the same thing about that novel you've been working on for five years. You're a dreamer, and I'm a realist. Dreams will not give us a new hot water heater and the million other things we need for this house. And now, on top of it all, I'm driving to an office on the other side of the city, and Jo is being forced to go to a new school."

"And I have papers to grade in the other room. I came in for some coffee, and you started World War Three," Adam said.

"At least when you're giving your history of war lecture to your class this afternoon, you can tell them you fired the first shot!"

Jo was sick of it, and even the thought of being the new kid in school was better than listening to her parents go at it again. Just after she poured herself some juice, a commercial on her mom's iPad grabbed her attention.

Jo watched as a teenage boy rode his bike down a long street, then skidded to a stop in front of a massive black big-top tent. She bumped up the volume just in time to hear bold, rhythmic music as rapid-fire images filled the screen. Goosebumps crawled up her arms but couldn't tear her eyes away. She watched as hundreds of kids in black military uniforms marched in step to the strange, jangling music playing. Their precision was impressive and mind-boggling all at the same time. *Who are they supposed to be? And where are they marching to?*

The image on the screen shifted to war-torn terrain, similar to the turmoil and destruction she had viewed in her dad's work. In this new imagery, bombs exploded with devastating force, tearing apart the already ravaged landscape.

Suddenly, the loud music stopped, and the scene faded. A lilting melody began to play against a dark sky where glittering fire embers descended and formed an outline of a massive flag adorned with two jagged lightning bolts that each resembled an angular letter S.

Jo stood transfixed at the image on the screen and watched as the fire embers began to glow brightly, then fade, and then grow bright again. Several phrases started to pulse in concert with the embers. *"Become your best! Step up to the test." "Live the game. Game to live!"* The background melody took on a new, higher-pitched tone. In the middle of the screen, the logo for *THE BIG TOP DOMAIN* materialized, and through it stepped a tall man. He wore a gray, double-breasted jacket over a white shirt and black tie, along with black trousers and black leather shoes. His black hair matched his black eyes. He moved like a living shadow and leaned close to the camera. "Warriors … wanted!" he said in a commanding voice. The commercial blinked off, and the *Love It or List It* program was back on the screen.

Jo shook herself from her reverie and whispered, "Stupid ad." She tore her gaze away from the iPad, only to be confronted by the all-too-familiar sound of her parents' raised voices. This time, their disagreement centered on the broken pipe that had unleashed a deluge from the sink cabinet.

"Look! I'm standing in water!" Evelyn shouted.

"Why don't you move?" Adam replied.

Through gritted teeth, she countered, "The sink is leaking."

Jo tried to sneak out of the kitchen, but her mom noticed.

"Wait a minute, Jo. You haven't had breakfast."

"I've got a protein bar in my backpack," Jo said.

"I don't know why you insisted on riding the bus your first day," her mom said. "I wanted to take you."

"I may as well start my new normal today," Jo said.

"Alright, but it's chilly outside," Mom said. "Take your jacket."

Jo plucked her jacket from a hook on the wall and put it on. Her dad watched her with a frown.

"You sure about the bus, munchkin? Maybe a ride to school can help calm the nerves a little?"

"I'm really not nervous," she lied.

Her dad went to the plate of pancakes stacked near the stove and tossed her one like a frisbee. "Here. And have a good day!"

Jo caught it easily and smiled. "Thanks." She slipped one shoulder strap of her backpack on and left through the kitchen door.

Chapter 2

Things Are Always Happening to Me

The yellow bus pulled into the bus bay in front of Robert Frost Middle School. As the other kids hurried off the bus, Jo remained in her seat. She missed her old bus, her old school, and especially her old friends. Everything felt unfamiliar now, including the driver's face reflected in the large rear-view mirror. The now-quiet bus allowed her to hear him clearly when he spoke.

"Everything okay?" he asked.

Jo nodded. "Yes. Sorry. Just going." As she made her way up the aisle to the door, he smiled at her.

"There's only one first day, you know. Tomorrow you'll be part of the gang."

Jo tried to smile back. "Thanks."

She made her way carefully down the bus steps. The last thing she needed was one of her annoying dizzy spells on the first day at a new school. Kids were streaming into the red brick building. The brave face she'd put on in front of her parents had been a lie. Inside, her stomach was doing somersaults as she made her way into the school.

Once inside, Jo pulled the paper with her new class schedule from the pocket of her jeans and studied it.

"First period … math," she mumbled. "That sums up my day."

She started walking down the hall and looked at the numbers above the doors. Someone bumped into her from behind; someone else brushed past her. "Go a little slower, why don't 'cha?" a boy said. A furious blush crept up her cheeks. She needed help, and she needed it fast. The bell for first period was about to ring, and the last thing she wanted was to walk into class late. She glanced around at the students in the hallway. A few feet away, a red-headed girl with a face filled with freckles had stopped to tuck something into her backpack. *She looks nice.*

Jo approached her. "Hi. Sorry to bother you, but it's my first day here."

The girl smiled. "Hi. I'm Polly Preston."

Jo returned the smile, relieved her instincts about this girl had been correct. "I'm Jo March. And I'm lost."

Polly held out her hand. "Let's see your schedule."

Jo handed it over, and Polly studied it. "Hey! You're in my third-period science class."

"Good. At least one face will be familiar," Jo said.

Polly offered a sympathetic smile. "Before you know it, everyone will be familiar. You'll see. Now, let's get you to your first class. And your second-period class is two doors down from that."

As they walked down the hall, Polly looked at her. "Jo March, huh? *Little Women* is one of my all-time favorite books!"

"Me too," Jo said. "And thanks for helping me."

"Of course," Polly said. She stopped at a classroom door. "Here you go. I'll save you a seat in science."

Jo stood at the threshold of her first-period class, watching as kids milled around, but the teacher was nowhere to be seen. She hesitated, her dad's advice echoing in her mind. *Just be yourself, Jo, and don't wait for them to notice you—make them notice you!*

Jo took a couple of steps inside and tried the same tactic she'd used to approach Polly. There were two pretty girls in cheerleader uniforms laughing together. *They seem nice.* Jo hoped she looked more confident than she felt as she approached them.

"Hi," Jo said.

They stopped and stared at her and, for a moment, almost looked annoyed. Jo's heart sank. *So ... maybe not so nice.* But then one of the girls smiled warmly. "Hi. We heard a new kid would be joining our class."

Relief. Jo smiled. "That's me. The new kid. I'm Jo."

"I'm Rosemary. Rose to my friends," she said, "and this is Carrie."

"Hi," Carrie said. "Welcome to Frost Middle School."

"Thanks," Jo said.

Rose leaned toward Jo. "Math is kinda lame, but Mr. Lupin is nice, and we get away with murder in here. He doesn't even care if we use our phones. Wait, you have a phone—right?" When Jo nodded, Rose held out her hand. "Give it here, and I'll put my info in it."

Jo hesitated and then dug her phone from the front pocket of her backpack. She entered the code to unlock it and handed it to Rose, who started to tap in her contact information.

Jo unzipped her jacket. "It seems awfully warm in here."

Carrie nodded. "The only downside to Mr. Lupin is that he's as old as dirt and keeps the thermostat as hot as my grandma's house."

Jo slipped her jacket off, and Carrie smiled. "Cute shirt!"

Jo looked down at her blue T-shirt, which said: *Bookmarks are for Quitters!* "Thanks." Jo pointed to a wide, silver bangle bracelet on Carrie's wrist. "I like your bracelet."

Carrie gestured to her uniform. "Me and Rose are co-captains of the cheer squad. We wear our uniforms on game days and for pep assemblies. I'm not supposed to wear jewelry with my uniform. I mean, sometimes I just want to wear a fun, cute shirt like yours, but no—I'm stuck in this thing."

Jo looked at Rose, who was still busy with her phone.

"I'm sure it's fun to be on the cheer squad, though, isn't it?" Jo asked.

"Well, yeah. I plan to cheer all the way through high school," Carrie said. "Do you do sports or band or anything?"

"Um, no. At my old school, I was on the yearbook staff and newspaper," Jo said.

Rose handed back her phone. "Where did you move from?"

"South Boston. I went to Whittier," Jo said.

"I've gone to school with the same kids since kindergarten," Carrie said.

"Me too," Jo said. "Till now."

"I'm sure you miss your friends," Rose said. "But you'll make new friends here. Like us, right, Carrie?"

Carrie smiled. "Right."

Jo relaxed. "Thanks."

Mr. Lupin entered the room. "Okay, everyone, take your seats." He looked at Jo and motioned for her to join him. "Joanna?"

Carrie and Rose flashed one more smile at Jo and then went to their respective desks while Jo reluctantly walked to the front of the class. Mr. Lupin sat on the edge of his desk.

"Like I mentioned last week, we have a new student joining our class today. This is Joanna…"

"Jo," she said quietly.

"Okay, this is *Jo* March. I expect everyone to make her feel welcome and help her out while she settles into the routine of our school. We have assigned seating in here, Jo. Your desk is the empty seat in the third row over there." He pointed at a desk about halfway down the aisle. She felt everyone's eyes on her as she made her way to her seat. Already self-conscious, Jo put her phone on her desk and her backpack on the floor. As soon as she sat down, a huge puff of white powder erupted. At the same time, a whoopee cushion produced the loudest fart, echoing through the room like a mighty roar from a mythical beast. Everyone in the class burst out laughing, and instant tears stung her eyes.

"Who did that?" Mr. Lupin demanded. The kids continued to giggle. Jo wanted to die but didn't move from her chair. She looked around and noticed Rose and Carrie grinning from ear to ear. *Well, Dad, I made them notice me.*

"I apologize for the immaturity of my class, Jo. Would you like to clean up your … the powder from your … pants?"

"No. I'm fine, thanks," she lied. *Second lie of the day. I'm on a roll.* She pulled the whoopee cushion from her seat revealing a mess the white baby powder had made all over her. She didn't need a mirror to know the butt of her jeans would look like she'd sat in a dozen powdered doughnuts. *Fake nice girls. The worst kind.*

The kids settled down, and Mr. Lupin launched into the algebraic equation for the day. Jo wanted to check on Nimble but didn't dare call more attention to herself. And then her phone speaker blasted Van Halen's "Hot for Teacher." "Got it bad! Got it bad! Got it bad! I'm hot for teacher!" The kids, once again, became nearly hysterical with laughter. Mr. Lupin strode toward Jo as she fumbled to get the music off her phone. Jo glanced up to see Rose grinning at her and waving her own phone in the air.

"I don't allow the use of your cell in here, Jo," he said. With trembling hands, she finally muted the song. "I didn't … it wasn't me," she mumbled. He held out his hand. "I'll hold on to it until class is over." Completely miserable and humiliated, she gave him the phone and folded her hands on top of her desk.

Rose spoke up. "Don't be too hard on her, Mr. Lupin. They probably allowed phones at her old school. Right, Joanna?" Heads swiveled to stare at her once again, but Jo smiled sweetly at Rose. "Right, Rosemary …" she mouthed, "baby." With a sneer at Jo, Rose turned back around, and Jo looked at the white knuckles on her hands, still tightly clenched together. Hour one at the new school, and she was ready to be a drop-out.

Chapter 3

Stuff Your Eyes with Wonder

Jo sat alone at a table in the corner of the bustling cafeteria during the lunch hour. The constant chatter filled the air, reminiscent of her old school. Kids crowded long tables, animatedly discussing their day, while others leaned over their phones, engrossed in videos that extracted bursts of laughter. Despite the noise, she ached with loneliness as she observed the camaraderie swirling around her.

She leaned down to where Nimble sat, hidden from view, in the open flap of her backpack. "What do you think they're laughing about, Nimble? That tale of my powdered butt is probably the stuff of legends by now." The little mouse gazed up at her with a serious expression, his whiskers twitching. She offered him a tiny piece of cheddar, and he sat back on his hind legs to nibble contently. "On a scale of one to ten for sucky days," she continued, sighing, "this one's hitting an eight already, and I still have two classes left!" She offered him another piece of cheese. "You're so lucky to be a mouse. No parents who fight all the time, no new house that reeks of mustiness, and no new school full of mean girls who pretend to be nice! No sneaky disease that makes your world spin without warning. No worries at all."

Jo glanced at the white, round clock on the wall and groaned. It felt like time was standing still. All she wanted was for the day to end so she could retreat to her room and escape from everything. As she looked away from the clock, she caught a glimpse of Rose and Carrie grinning in her direction. Jo quickly averted her eyes and spotted Polly waving. *No eye contact! No eye contact!* Pretending she hadn't seen her, Jo turned back to give Nimble another small piece of cheese. "She seemed nice, Nimble, but for all I know, Polly might be as phony as Carrie and Rose. She was way too bubbly in science class. No one likes science that much!" Nimble finished his cheese, and just as Jo was about to give him one last piece, Polly and another girl walked toward her. Jo hurriedly lowered the flap of her backpack to conceal Nimble just as the girls approached the table.

"Hi, Jo," Polly said. "This is Sara."

Jo greeted the petite brunette beside Polly. Sara offered a big smile that showed off a mouth full of braces that gave her a pronounced lisp.

"Hi, Jo. Ith nicth to meet you."

"Why don't you join us, Jo?" Polly gestured to a table in the back of the room. "I figure a name like Jo March and a T-shirt like the one you're wearing means you're a book lover. And we just happen to have a book club that meets at lunch. We're not a big group, but we have some lively discussions about the books we read."

Jo hesitated. "Um, I don't know …" *I already trusted two girls this morning, and look how that turned out. Besides, I've got Nimble to think of. …*

"Our book this month was kind of a sweet one," Polly said.

Sara raised her eyebrows. "Thweet? You're kidding? It ith not thweet."

Polly shrugged off Sara's comment. "I can find something happy and sweet in almost anything. The book is *Fahrenheit 451* by Ray Bradbury. Do you know it?"

Jo nodded. "I think Bradbury was the greatest science-fiction writer of his time. He wrote that book over fifty years ago and practically had a crystal ball into the future. Our future. Like the way he wrote that whole newspaper articles would become nothing more than a sentence or two and that technology would make imagination and critical thinking obsolete." She glanced around the cafeteria at the kids glued to their phones. "I guess even he didn't think that conversation would also be a thing of the past because of technology."

Polly and Sara exchanged glances. "Wow," Polly said. "I wish those guys had heard you say that. They'd be impressed."

Jo looked toward the table in the back where two boys were sitting.

"The rotund boy with the pocket protector in hith thhirt ith Jake," Sara said. "If you ever want to know a thatithtic about anything … and I do mean anything … Jake ith your guy."

Jo nodded. "He's in my math class. He answered a lot of questions today."

"Noah is the other one in our club. Even though he's African American, he identifies as Harry Potter. I don't even think he needs those big round glasses, but he never takes them off."

"So? What do you say? No one wants to eat alone—am I right?" Polly asked.

"We heard about what Carrie and Rothe did to you today. That wath tho mean," Sara said.

Polly looked in the direction of the cheerleaders. "Rose and Carrie, pretty faces but rotten inside. I keep trying to find some redeeming quality about them, but so far … well, I'm still trying. But most of the kids here are really nice."

"Oh, oh," Sara said. "Look who ith bugging Jake and Noah."

The girls turned to see a hulk of a boy wearing a football jersey taunting Noah and Jake by holding a copy of a paperback in the air and waving it back and forth.

"Is that another one of the *nice* kids at this school?" Jo asked.

"Unfortunate timing," Sara said. "That ith Cleet. He belongth in the Carrie and Roseth club."

Sara yelled loudly, "Leave them alone, Cleet!"

Cleet looked in their direction and yelled back. "Here you go, losers! Fetch!" He launched the book, and it sailed through the air, landing right next to Jo's backpack.

To Jo's horror, the crash of the book spooked Nimble, causing him to dart out from under the flap of the backpack. He scurried across the back of Polly's hand and leaped off the table.

Polly screamed. "Was that a mouse?!"

Jo didn't take the time to answer. She sprang to her feet and took off after Nimble.

Chapter 4

Embrace the Madness

Jo caught glimpses of Nimble's green vest as he darted around, skillfully navigating between people's feet. Chaos ensued, with screams following in his wake. Jo's heart raced with fear at the thought of losing her beloved companion. That outcome would be too devastating to bear. He was the one thing that felt familiar and normal. *I was so selfish to bring him with me today.* She vowed that once she caught him, she'd never bring him to school again.

Someone yelled at the top of their lungs, "Eeks! Get away from me!"

Jo turned to see that bully Cleet swing a lunch tray like a flyswatter at Nimble, but the little mouse was quicker and scampered up the boy's pant leg. Cleet issued a loud, high-pitched squeal, hitting a vocal note of E7. He shimmied around until Nimble slipped out the bottom of his pants and scrambled away. Frantic fear took over, and the girls jumped onto tables and chairs, with everyone keeping their eyes peeled for the furry little rodent. Jo lost sight of Nimble as he ducked around a table leg and disappeared.

Jo swept her gaze around the latest area of leaping, scared kids, and spotted Nimble.

"Please, please, please … just stay put," she whispered.

As she raced toward Nimble, he ran toward Carrie and Rose. The girls shrieked in unison. Terrified of the little mouse, Carrie leaped onto the table and flipped her lunch tray onto the floor. Her silver bracelet slid off her wrist and started to roll. Rose tried to scramble onto the table but lost her footing and fell, bottom first, into the lunch tray with a half-eaten, saucy ground-beef sandwich.

As Jo passed Rose, she couldn't help herself. "You've got a little sloppy me on your butt."

Rose growled, "Somebody's going to pay for this!"

Nimble jumped into the rolling bracelet and started to run as if he were on his exercise wheel. She made a dive for him under the next table, just missing as Nimble rolled out the other side. "Nimble!" she hissed at him. "Come back here!" She crawled out from under the table and stood too fast. The world tilted, and she swayed. *No, no, no! Not now! Please, not now!*

But the wheels were in motion, and her balance was off, and she knew she was going down. Just as her knees buckled and she began to descend to the floor, a strong pair of arms caught her, effortlessly halting her tumble. Breathless, she looked up, her gaze meeting the striking face of a handsome boy, mere inches away, close enough for an accidental kiss.

The boy frowned. "You okay?"

"Huh?"

He brushed back long, blond bangs from his forehead and studied her. "I said, are you okay?"

"Yeah," she said. "I just stood up too fast. I've got Meniere's Disease."

"Never heard of it."

"It's an inner ear thing. Dizziness, vertigo. Stuff like that." Her eyes drifted past him to the bracelet rolling across the floor, capturing her full attention. "Thanks for saving me."

Upon her return from the restroom, Miss Matilda Windsor, typically a composed and tranquil lunch monitor, was caught off-guard by the chaotic scene unfolding before her. While she would often intervene with a gentle reprimand if the students grew too boisterous in the cafeteria, the current situation had left her completely unhinged. She was both shocked and baffled at the pandemonium in what was usually a very orderly, composed lunch hour.

"What is it?!" she yelled over the noise. "What in heaven's name is the matter?"

As Matilda Windsor looked for the source of the chaos, the runaway silver bracelet headed her way. When it got close enough, she put out her sensible white shoe and stopped it. In one swift motion, Ms. Windsor plucked the bracelet off the floor, only to discover a startled mouse nestled within. A shriek escaped her lips as she instinctively flung the unexpected visitor against the nearby wall.

Jo watched in horror as the bracelet crashed to the floor, releasing the motionless form of little Nimble. As the class bell chimed, signaling the end of lunch, a surge of students jumped off the tables and chairs and hurried for the cafeteria exit. Amidst the chaotic rush, Jo hurried toward Nimble. Over the commotion, Miss Windsor's voice pierced through as she urgently relayed a message over her walkie-talkie, requesting the custodian's help in addressing the rodent problem.

Jo's heart hammered with dread as she gently cradled her furry friend. She whispered urgently, "Stay with me, please ..." as she hurriedly made her way out of the cafeteria.

Hidden behind the door of a stall in the girls' bathroom, Jo tried hard to keep her tears at bay while she gently stroked the back of the little mouse. "Please, Nimble. *Please*. I need you."

Jo raised her palm to her lips, gently blew air into his face, and continued to stroke his back. "Please, Nimble ... come back to life." At first, she didn't believe her own eyes when his whiskers moved. And then his little nose twitched. Eyes opened and regarded her with curiosity.

Jo nearly shouted with joy. "Nimble. You're alive!"

She took a few seconds to just hold him and let her heartbeat return to normal.

"Sometimes the smallest things take up the most room in your heart," she whispered.

A sharp rap on the stall door nearly made Jo drop Nimble again. "We know you're in there, Joanna!"

Jo looked down at two sets of feet clad in identical tennis shoes with pompoms on the toes. Cheerleaders.

"Um, a little privacy, please," Jo said.

But the girls continued to talk to her through the stall door.

"Me and Rose know that was your mouse that caused all that chaos in the cafeteria," Carrie said.

"I don't know what you're talking about," Jo said.

"We found the evidence," Carrie said.

Jo watched as her backpack came sliding under the stall door, with Nimble's cage riding on top.

"So gross. Who brings a rodent to school?" Rose said.

"A total dork loser, that's who," Carrie suggested. The girls laughed as Jo watched their shoes under the door.

"Please leave me alone," Jo said.

"Oh, we'll leave you alone, alright," Rose said. "We're going to tell Miss Windsor why her spotless cafeteria is now a flipping mess. Tommy Spencer brought a lizard to school last year, and he got a three-day suspension for letting it loose in science class."

"Way to make an impression, new girl," Rose said. "And by the way, you'll be getting a bill from my parents to get my skirt cleaned."

Like a choreographed cheer routine, both pairs of tennis shoes pivoted and disappeared. Jo waited until she heard the bathroom door close and lifted Nimble up to eye level.

"Rose's butt covered in Sloppy Joe … possible detention? Totally worth it."

Chapter 5
The Dark Is Rising

The school bus inched through the busy Boston streets. Sitting alone in the front, Jo opened her backpack to peek at Nimble. The mouse had been her constant companion for over a year. When she'd told her parents she wanted a mouse, they pushed back with the usual arguments about getting a pet, but she argued she didn't have a dog, or a cat, or even a bird. Was it too much to ask to have one tiny mouse? In the end, her parents gave in, and they took her to the pet store to find a mouse.

As she perused the cages filled with mice, one stood on his hind legs with his front paws on the glass, and Jo could have sworn he winked at her. She loved him instantly. She named him Nimble and was sure he'd be every bit as smart and precocious as the Nimble in author Dorothy Kilner's book, *The Life and Perambulations of a Mouse*. The book, originally published in 1784, was one of her prized possessions.

Her Nimble would have made his namesake proud. He was excellent company. He listened to all her hopes, dreams, and fears and never judged her. Jo knew he was annoyed at her for caging him again, but as she'd tried to explain to him, it was for his own good and safety. How many times had she heard that from her parents? Too many to count. *Jo … don't run. It's not safe for you. You could fall again.* Meniere's was no joke, and she knew it made them worry about her all the time. Worry. She had plenty of that right now. Every time they opened their mouths, she was afraid of what they might say. *Just because we're having some problems, you know we will always love you. Our issues have nothing to do with you, Jo.*

Nimble was fast asleep in his cage. *Let's face it. It's not every day you're brought back from the dead,* she thought. Jo only hoped he'd learned something from it. He was an unusually smart, intuitive mouse and her best friend. He had to stay safe. Her dad's voice popped into her head: *"We just want you to be safe, Jo. We love you."*

While the surrounding kids joked and chatted, Jo pulled her phone from her backpack and scrolled through the pictures—until she came to her very favorite one. It was an old photo taken on a camping trip. They were in front of a small cabin with a sparkling lake in the background. Her eight-year-old self was beaming between the smiling faces of her parents. It had been a wonderful trip filled with adventures and so many memories. *Memories …* she thought. *They warm you up from the inside. But they also tear you apart.* With a sigh, she shoved her phone into her backpack. The bus braked at an intersection. Jo looked out the window at the police officer who had stepped into the street to direct traffic. *Must be an accident, or maybe a traffic light is out.*

The police officer was holding traffic to allow a caravan of jet-black semi-trucks to make the turn at the intersection. One by one, the trucks rolled past, their heavily tinted windows ensuring privacy for the drivers inside. Each black trailer bore the same bold logo painted on the side—an image of the man from the Big Top Domain commercial, now taking on an eerily lifelike presence. He stood proudly in the center of a dramatic double-lightning bolt flag, arms outstretched as if welcoming them. His gaze seemed to come alive, locking onto Jo with an unsettling intensity. Jo shivered. *Those eyes seem like they're piercing right through me.*

And then, as the last two trucks crept past in the slithering parade of black, two glowing, yellow orbs shined through the cab's tinted windows. Surprised, she snapped her head back from the window. She turned in her seat to watch the end of the procession. The last two red taillights of the semis disappeared, leaving behind a bruised, darkening sky and wind gusts that rocked the streetlights. The October trees shuddered in the wind and gave up their leaves. She leaned her forehead against the glass and watched the wind whip things into a frenzy. Though she wasn't cold, Jo shivered. "Something wicked this way comes."

That evening, during dinner, it was clear to Jo her parents were attempting to show a united front. They asked lots of questions about her day, the new people she'd met, and even the bus ride to and from school. Jo assured them everything was fine. She told them she'd joined a book club, which made them happy. She was careful not to mention what a disaster the day had really been. Lucky for her, Miss Windsor gave her some grace about Nimble, and she wasn't faced with detention or suspension. Just a couple of lunch hours helping the custodian do his job during the week. It was a fair punishment, and she didn't plan to worry her parents about it. Just like she didn't tell them about the powdered butt, whoopee cushion fart, snarky girls, runaway almost-dead mouse, and creepy truck procession through town. As soon as she was able, she excused herself and said she wanted to get started on homework.

"I was thinking it's time for a family meeting," her mom said, carefully avoiding her dad's eyes. Jo shook her head. "Can't tonight, Mom. I'm already behind at this school and want to get caught up."

"Your dad and I really do want to talk to you, Jo," her mom said. "I think it's important we're all on the same page."

Jo didn't say the first thing that came to mind: *I'm pretty sure it's not a page I'm going to like.* Instead, she forced a smile. "As long as it's not something that's going to occupy my mind instead of the homework I have to do." She watched her mom and dad exchange a look, and then her mom nodded. "Okay, sweetie. It can wait. You get started on that homework of yours." Relieved, Jo hurried up the stairs before they could change their minds. A family meeting was code for:

We are going to tell you something you don't want to hear. The bickering between Mom and Dad had intensified into full-blown arguments, evolving into a tense cold war that sometimes lasted for days. Jo realized things had worsened; they could no longer keep it under wraps. What used to be whispered, heated discussions behind closed doors were now spilling out in her presence more frequently. If they were contemplating something drastic like separation or divorce, she figured it couldn't happen if they couldn't tell her. If she could stall them long enough, maybe things would work themselves out.

Outside, a storm was building. Inside, Jo sat at her desk under the window in her room and chewed the end of her pen. With a frustrated sigh, she looked down at the blank sheet of notebook paper. "Just one word, Jo. Any word. Just start!" Instead of a word, she drew a big circle with a frowning face inside. On one side of her desk, she had a framed quote from author Virginia Woolf: "A woman must have money and a room of her own if she is to write fiction." She turned her attention to a pile of books on the corner of her desk: *Hidden Figures, The Outsiders, Harry Potter.* "I've got two hundred dollars saved and my own room, and I still can't seem to get started. How did you guys do it?" Jo shifted her gaze to Nimble, perched on top of the books, while he tended to his nightly ritual of washing his tiny paws.

"Nimble, by the time I write my first book, even *The Never Ending Story* will have ended." He peeked at her, then went back to his grooming. A bright, jagged lightning bolt split the sky right outside Jo's window. "Uh, oh. This will be loud!" Jo exclaimed as she reached for Nimble, just as a deafening crash of thunder reverberated overhead. Startled, Nimble leaped off the stack of books and made a beeline for the vent in the floor. Jo quickly shoved her chair back and raced after him.

"No, Nimble! Stop! Stop!" But before she could reach him, Nimble disappeared into the vent. Jo yanked the vent cover off. Grabbing her phone, she used the flashlight to peer into the dark recesses. "Crazy mouse … crazy, crazy, crazy mouse!" The vent went to the floor below, so she ran downstairs and hurried into an empty room her parents used as a temporary storeroom. Moving boxes were piled in one corner, and an enormous piece of furniture covered with a white tarp was against one wall. Jo pulled off that vent cover and was surprised that the vent led to another floor below. Nimble was squeaking from below. *That can't be possible. I'm on the first floor … there's nothing below here.* Nimble squeaked again, but Jo couldn't see him in the flashlight's beam. "I'm coming, Nimble. I'll get you out of there."

But *where* was there? Jo had no idea since there was no basement in the house. At least that's what they'd been told. She looked frantically around the room to find some kind of solution to her problem. She couldn't fit down the vent, but she could drop something to Nimble. Maybe a rope? Or maybe some kind of string she could thread into the vent, and Nimble could climb up to her. Jo checked all the boxes for anything she could use, but there was nothing.

The only thing she hadn't checked was under the tarp of the large piece of furniture that had come with the house. Maybe there was something in there she could use to rescue Nimble from the vent. She pulled hard on the white tarp and watched as a massive mahogany piece of furniture was revealed. Jo stared at it in wonder when she realized that carved into the wood were pictures of various classic children's books.

Immediately, what came to mind was C. S. Lewis, *The Lion, The Witch and the Wardrobe.* Jo opened the door and stepped inside the vast space. She used her phone's flashlight and shined it all over the interior, but nothing looked out of the ordinary.

"Get a grip, Jo," she said to herself. "Did you really think you were going to find a hidden door leading to another land?" Jo could barely make out Nimble's little squeak from somewhere beyond. She banged her hand in frustration against the back of the wardrobe, only to hear a hollow thud. Not at all what she'd expected. More than a little curious, Jo ran her fingers down the back wall and stopped when she came across a small piece of wood that felt different from the rest. She pressed the wood, and suddenly, the back of the wardrobe swung open and revealed a staircase.

"No way …" Jo sucked in her breath. She bounced her flashlight around the stairway but couldn't tell anything about where it might lead. Nimble squeaked again, louder and closer. "I'm coming,

Nimble. I'm coming!" She was nervous but determined to save her little mouse. Jo started down the dark stairs ... one creaking step at a time.

Chapter 6

Let My Heart Be Still

Even as Jo descended, the storm continued to rage. *This is stupid. Heading down into total darkness to who knows where. Good thing I love that little mouse.* She got to the bottom of the stairs and shined the flashlight in the immediate vicinity around her, hoping to find a light switch. There was nothing but space. Dark, seemingly endless space.

"Nothing creepy about this," she mumbled. "Nimble? Where are you?"

She scrunched her nose at the strange odors surrounding her—musty, dusty, and something that was hard to pinpoint. *Can 'old' be a smell?* She felt instant relief at Nimble's familiar squeak to her left. She arced the light in that direction and was delighted to find the little mouse sitting up, looking back at her.

"Nimble! There you are! Don't you dare move a muscle!" She hurried toward him and scooped him up. "That's twice in one day, my little friend. Quit bolting!" She opened her hand, and he scampered up her arm and perched on her shoulder. She swung her light in front of her, illuminating a red brick wall. Taking a few steps forward, she swept the beam across shelves secured to the brick. They were stocked with bottles, mason jars, reams of paper, and neatly folded white towels. Beneath the shelves hung various tools on hooks—saws, hammers, paintbrushes, and levels. Farther along, there were two large chalkboards mounted next to the shelves, their green surfaces filled with equations and scientific theories scribbled in white chalk.

"What is this place, Nimble? Do Mom and Dad know it's here and just didn't tell me?" The thought of exploring the entire basement was fleeting; in the darkness, she couldn't gauge the size of the space or what might be lurking within it. Both unknowns made her anxious.

"Maybe we should get out of here," she suggested to Nimble. "There might be an axe murderer down here, watching our every move." She chuckled nervously. "I've definitely read too many Edgar Allan Poe stories." Another arc of her flashlight, and she caught a long wooden worktable in the beam. "But maybe we should check that out first." With Nimble perched on her shoulder, Jo approached the worktable. She shifted her light slowly from one end to the other, marveling at all the different items before her. Bottles and beakers, a microscope, and an old-fashioned-looking scale for measuring. There were also baskets with different colors of clay, acrylic paints, beeswax, sculpting tools, fabric remnants, and even what appeared to be human hair. Almost everything looked old and out of date. *Talk about a man-cave. Or woman-cave. Or mad-scientist lab.* And then she spotted something that truly interested her—a large book that lay open on the table.

"Whoa … look at this!"

As she pulled the book closer, Nimble ran down her arm and sat attentively as she inspected the handwritten page.

"Listen to this, Nimble." Jo read the first passage on the page aloud. *"The stolen innocence of childhood haunts my every waking moment. I believe that the characters I've created are my way of giving joy back to children. Back to what should have been the great-great-grandchildren of those I took it from."*

Jo kept her finger on the page but closed the book to see intricate, hand-tooled designs etched into a leather cover.

"Beautiful, but no title. Maybe someone's diary or journal?" She opened it again and flipped to the next page, where there was another handwritten passage.

"Music has become a necessary part of my creative process. It provides comfort in the moments when I believe myself to be slipping into insanity. I also think the friends I've created enjoy the melody and find comfort in the notes as much as I do. For without music, life would be a mistake."

"That's one way to get friends. Just create them. Why haven't I thought of that?"

She flipped another page and gasped in surprise at a very detailed drawing of Dorothy Gale, exactly as the author had described her in *The Wonderful Wizard of Oz*. At her feet was a basket with a little black dog inside. "Oh my gosh, Dorothy! And Toto! You're perfect." Chill bumps ran up her arms as she turned page after page, each with a drawing of beloved characters from her favorite books. Alongside Dorothy, there were the Scarecrow, Tin Woodman, and the Cowardly Lion, as well as Pinocchio, Snow White, Robin Hood, Aladdin, the Reluctant Dragon, and many others.

"They all look just as I imagine when I read the stories! So ..." Jo furrowed her brows as she shook her head. "The friends the author of this journal wrote about are just pictures?"

Nimble regarded her with twitching whiskers. "Of course, I know you can't just create friends, Nimble. But one can wish ..."

Jo turned another page and kept reading.

"My miraculous elixir, shrouded in an aura of ancient secrets and untold power, holds the key to bridging the vast chasm between life and death—to animate the inanimate. However, my theory is that the ethereal fluid must harness the potent forces of lightning to defy the finality of death. With nature's fury embodied within its electric veins, this mystical elixir will hopefully dance with the energy of a lightning storm and breathe life into the silent heart to beat once more. I will call it the Powder of Life."

Jo frowned. "Defy death? Harness lightning? What the heck is the Powder of Life?"

A loud, rolling drumbeat of thunder crashed outside, and Jo

jumped. "We should probably get going, Nimble. Just in case Mom or Dad are looking for me."

But instead of moving, she looked back at the journal. "Maybe just a couple minutes more …" She turned a few more pages and stopped. Her eyes widened at the next drawing of a man, which didn't seem to fit with the rest. She studied the details the artist had included. The subject of the drawing wore a dark greenish-gray thigh-length tunic over dark trousers. A silver, braided belt was around his waist, and medals adorned his chest. His rank and insignia were of someone high in command. Jo knew from her lengthy history lessons with her dad that this was a drawing of an officer in the Third Reich. "Why include a drawing of a German officer in this journal?" She finally looked closely at the officer's face and shook her head. "Wait. This can't be right. He looks exactly like the creepy guy on the trucks and in the commercial." She traced her finger down to the words written under the drawing.

"I will not write down his name. I won't give him that distinction. There is only one reason I'm attempting to give him life. He is the vessel into which I've poured all my selfish, dark, evil, and prideful thoughts. A place to hold all that is wrong with me so that I will become innocent and pure and, therefore, worthy of the friends I've created. He will be a substitute on my behalf and be judged for my crimes against humanity. The lethal testing of subjects at children's clinics throughout Germany and Austria. When I find him guilty, I will sentence him to death, along with my sin that he will carry for eternity."

Jo kept her eyes on the drawing. "The author wanted to bring him to life so he could kill him? *Life is infinitely stranger than anything the mind of man could invent.*" She shuddered. "Even Sherlock Holmes would have a hard time with this one. Crimes against humanity? Lethal injections? All those children during Hitler's reign?" She swallowed hard. "Oh my gosh, those poor children and what they endured."

Another loud crash of thunder caused Nimble to jump and scurry back up Jo's arm. She closed the journal and picked it up to take with her. "Let's get out of here. This is all too creepy for me."

Jo retraced her path to the stairs and tried not to rush as she climbed up to the first floor, even as her imagination told her the unknown author of the journal could be nipping at her heels.

Chapter 7

Not All Those Who Wander Are Lost

Jo woke the next morning thinking about her discovery the night before. She couldn't decide if it was more creepy than exciting or more exciting than creepy. A secret basement in an old house, obviously used decades ago by someone who loved children's classic books and *vengeance*. As she was putting on her jeans and a t-shirt, Jo revisited an argument she'd had with herself since she'd discovered the hidden world downstairs. When to tell her parents. She knew it should be right away—this morning before school. But then they would explore without her, and she hated that thought. She wanted to be with them when they saw it for the first time. Maybe she'd gauge their moods and then decide when to tell them. And then it occurred to her. Something was off—different this morning. *No arguing! Actual quiet!* She felt a flicker of optimism. *Maybe today will be a really good day.*

She gathered her things together and then went to say goodbye to Nimble. The little mouse stared at her.

"Don't look at me like that," she said. "You can't come with me today. I'm sorry, but I can't risk anything happening to you. You'll have plenty of time to run around when I get home."

Nimble turned his back on her and burrowed into the cedar shavings of his little habitat.

Jo entered the quiet kitchen. The first thing she saw were two suitcases sitting next to the back door. The second thing she noticed was both of her parents at the table, coffee mugs in front of them, serious expressions on their faces.

Jo felt a stab of unease. "Good morning."

"Morning, munchkin," her dad said.

"Morning, sweetie," her mom answered.

Jo looked pointedly at the suitcases. "Someone taking a trip?"

"We need to have a little talk," Mom said, her voice trembling slightly. "Can I get you some juice or breakfast first?"

Jo shook her head as she looked at her mom, who seemed both familiar and foreign.

"The suitcases are mine, Jo. Your dad and I have decided it's best if we don't live together right now."

Jo's eyes immediately filled with tears. "Right now? Or forever?"

Her mom and dad looked at each other. *Who is going to be brave enough to answer me?*

Her dad sighed. "Look, munchkin, we haven't made any permanent decisions. But I know you realize things have been … tense lately. There are things we need to work out, and all the arguing and day-to-day stresses aren't helping. Sometimes people just need time apart to figure out how to come back together."

"You mean *if* they come back together?" Jo asked, her lips quivering.

"Like your dad said, we haven't made a permanent decision. But things have gotten to a point where it's unhealthy for me—and him—and especially you to continue living this way. I'm going to stay with my friend Shelly for a little while. You and Dad will be here. We don't want to disrupt your life."

With each moment, Jo felt smaller, as if the world around her was expanding while she shrank into a corner of her own heart, trying to comprehend this new reality. No longer did she feel like the clever girl with dreams of adventure. Instead, she felt like a little child again, the innocence of youth eroding like sandcastles under the relentless tide. "I don't want to go to school today."

Her dad nodded. "Of course, you can stay home. I'll be here all day in my office doing Zoom calls with students."

Her mom got up and went to embrace her. Jo wanted to cling to her and beg her not to go, but instead, she stood stiffly and allowed her mom to hug her. "I'll see you every day. And you can text me anytime you want. And I love you, Jo. Very, very much."

She nodded mutely, grabbed her backpack from the floor, and ran back up the stairs to her room.

Jo slammed her bedroom door loud enough for her parents to hear it. She hoped it made them feel as bad as she felt. First, they moved her away from her friends and old school, and now this? It wasn't fair. She grabbed her phone, pulled up her playlist, and hit play. "Anywhere but Here" from the musical *Pretty Woman* came through the Bluetooth speaker on her dresser. The lyrics of the song seemed to fit her life lately. Not belonging, not fitting in, and not what she wanted at all. *"I know where I'd choose to go if I could disappear. Anywhere but here."* She cranked up the volume, walked to her window, and let the tears flow.

Jo leaned her forehead against the window's glass and saw the fast-approaching storm. She brushed impatiently at her wet cheeks. *Nature's fury.* Lightning in the distance lit up the dark clouds. *What did that journal say? Something about lightning …*

Desperately wanting to think of something besides her fracturing family, Jo lifted the mattress on her bed and pulled out the leather journal from the basement. She flipped through the pages until she found the passage: *harness the potent forces of lightning to defy the finality of death. With nature's fury embodied within its electric veins, this mystical elixir will hopefully dance with the energy of a lightning storm and breathe life into the silent heart to beat once more.*

How do you harness the potent forces of lightning? She turned another page and found the answer.

It was a drawing she'd missed the night before. This one was of a widow's walk perched on the roof—with a long lightning rod reaching toward the sky.

Jo knew, of course, that their house had a widow's walk. Her dad told her it was a dated architectural feature popular in the previous century.

Jo flipped back to the beautiful, detailed drawings of the characters. Each and every one had been lovingly sketched and looked as though they could step right off the page. However, after reading the journal, Jo had the distinct impression that it wasn't enough for the author. He wrote of friends he'd *created,* not drawn. She thought back to the things she'd seen in the basement. The wax, the paint, the fabric—the hair. *Breathe life into the silent heart.*

At that moment, Jo knew she would go back through the wardrobe and down the stairs. But first, she had to go up.

Jo left her music playing—loud enough for her dad to think she was soothing her sorrows in songs. She wasn't ready to let her dad in on her discovery of the secret basement just yet. And she certainly wasn't about to ask permission to go up to the widow's walk. Especially in an electrical storm. Better to ask for forgiveness later. The hallway that led to the widow's walk had a door that stayed closed. The trapdoor that led to the roof wasn't sealed as well as it should have been and was one of the many repairs that Mom said needed to be done. *"We may as well be heating the entire outside, Adam. Not exactly cost-effective to watch the heat rise up and out of the roof!"*

A long rope dangled from the trapdoor in the ceiling, and Jo tugged on it. Attic-type stairs came down, and she hurried up them before she lost her nerve. As she climbed, a noticeable drop in temperature enveloped her. *Mom might have been right about this one.* She shoved the door open, and immediately, the storm assaulted her. Determined to test her theory, she climbed through the doorway, ducking her head against the pelting rain. The lightning rod she'd hoped to see wasn't attached to the roof but was lying on the ground. From her vantage point, a spectacular light show was headed her way. She knew lifting a metal pole during an electrical storm wasn't the smartest thing to do, but she was undeterred. *Harness the forces of a lightning storm ... breathe life into the silent heart.*

Jo shoved the lightning rod into the metal slot on the roof. Instantly, the opening line of *Something Wicked This Way Comes* came to mind. "The seller of lightning rods arrived just ahead of the storm." She hurried back through the trapdoor.

Armed with the journal and an actual flashlight, Jo pushed down her unease at being back in the basement. The light from the flashlight offered some comfort, but her curiosity about the "friends" the journal's author had written about truly spurred her on.

Jo shined the light past the worktable into the dark abyss. There was a pathway on the cement floor made of yellow bricks. *Follow the yellow brick road?* It led to a large wooden door with an intricately carved stone structure decorated with ancient symbols and runes.

Stepping up to the door, Jo reached out to grasp the handle, but to no avail. The door remained stubbornly unmoved. Using her flashlight, she directed the beam upon the intricate symbols etched into the weathered surface. A sense of recognition washed over Jo as the realization struck her: this was reminiscent of the entrance to the legendary Mines of Moria. Whispers of ancient lore echoed in her mind as she murmured to herself, "Only those who know the secret password will gain entrance." She closed her eyes to conjure up the memory of the words that held the key. And then it came to her, and she tested the phrase.

"Speak, friend, and enter." As soon as the words left her lips, a resounding click reverberated through the air, followed by the door swinging open before her astonished eyes. As the induction coils awakened, infused with an electrical current generated by an electronic ballast, the ultraviolet waves traversed the phosphor coating. Like an artist's brushstroke on a canvas, the phosphor coating converted the ultraviolet waves into a vibrant spectrum of visible light, illuminating the surroundings with a soft, enchanting glow.

"Holy crap!"

Chapter 8
Whatever Our Souls Are Made Of

A full-sized wolf appeared to be in mid-stride, coming right for Jo. The sight of the fearsome wolf nearly took her breath away, and his lifelike appearance was staggering. She hesitated, then approached it. His eyes were penetrating, staring straight ahead at some unseen prey. Gathering her courage, Jo reached out and touched his fur. *Real! He's real! Or at least he was ...* This was the work of an excellent taxidermist.

Jo stepped around the wolf, her heart pounded with anticipation, as she realized who the "friends" were. She stepped toward her motionless audience and stopped to stare. Facing her were dozens of life-sized figures: a girl with long hair, a wooden boy, a dragon as big as a horse. The list went on and on. She made her way to the closest of the figures. "Robin Hood!" Jo hesitated before reaching up to touch Robin Hood's cheek. "Wax," she said. Next, she moved to a boy who looked like he'd come straight from China. She touched a large ring on his hand, which was wrapped around a small brass lamp. "Aladdin. I'd know you anywhere." Next to him was another boy, short in stature, wearing a loincloth. His knees and elbows were calloused, and his black hair was shaggy and draped low across his forehead. Jo studied him. "After losing your parents to a tiger attack, you were adopted by your wolf mother and father, who named you Mowgli, which means frog, because of your lack of fur and your refusal to sit still."

Next, Jo stood in front of a silver man holding an axe. He had short silver legs, a round silver body, and even a silver pointed hat perched on his very silver head. Tentatively, Jo reached out and touched the man's face.

"Tin." She smiled. "I know you, of course, Mr. Tin Woodman. But if you're here, that means …" Jo quickly moved on and stopped in front of a girl about her size, wearing a worn-looking blue-and-white gingham dress and silver shoes. She had a pink sunbonnet on her head and brown braids that hung halfway down her back. A basket at her feet with a small dog and an oil can inside made Jo laugh out loud. "I can't believe this. It's you! Dorothy Gale!" She gently touched Dorothy's wax cheek. "I've always dreamed of you and me being best friends! You look exactly like L. Frank Baum described you in his book." Jo stared in wonder. She reached out and smoothed a non-existent wrinkle from Dorothy's dress. "You're … perfect."

Her gaze swept over the room. "You're all perfect," she said reverently.

So amazed at her discovery, Jo had failed to notice a straight-backed wooden chair in the room. It had a leather seat and back and sat next to a small table that held an ancient-looking phonograph. The phonograph was housed in a small, brown suitcase. A long, silver handle protruded from the bottom of the case, and a vinyl record was on the turntable. *Music has become a necessary part of my creative process.* Jo set the needle on the record, then turned the crank. A beautiful, lilting melody started to play. There was something familiar about the tune, but she couldn't quite place it. Jo sat in the chair, looked at all the wax characters again, and wondered about the artist who'd created them. Someone with incredible talent and an obvious love of children's classic literature. The artist seemed to have had a particular affinity for the Oz characters. What an incredible imagination! She remembered one of her favorite quotes.

"Deep into that darkness peering, long I stood there," she whispered, "wondering, fearing, doubting, dreaming dreams no mortal ever dared to dream before."

With the music still playing, Jo stepped out of the enchanted room but still sensed a lingering atmosphere of magic and wonder. The air crackled with energy as the echoes of words she'd read from the classics still danced in her head. With these mystical remnants still fresh in her thoughts, she made her way back to the worktable.

"Somebody dared to dream up something this amazing." She turned another page in the journal, flipped past a drawing of her house, and finally found the page she'd glanced at the night before but hadn't really understood its relevance. But now she knew it was step-by-step instructions on how to make the Powder of Life.

Jo was suddenly grateful her parents had made her take a correspondence course in chemistry over the summer. *College is expensive, Jo … scholarships are awarded to those who put in the extra effort.* She read the list of ingredients: I-53 iodine; Ag 47 silver; Cu 29 Copper; Au 79 gold. She recalled something else from chemistry class. *Silver, copper, and gold are all conductors of electricity. And properly handled, it could change liquid to powder!*

What are the chances those ingredients are still here? She moved jars and bottles that were labeled with items she recognized: acetone, alcohol, distilled water, plasma, and formaldehyde. *Formaldehyde? Plasma?* But not the specific ingredients on the list.

She swung her flashlight across the worktable to make sure she hadn't missed anything and then bounced the beam across the brick wall with the shelves. The light reflected off some glass containers.

Jo made her way to the shelves and sucked in an excited breath. There they were. All the ingredients she needed. Referring to the instructions in the journal, Jo used the scale to mix equal portions of the gold, silver, and copper together in a metal bowl with handles she found on the worktable. She added a small amount of the distilled water and a spoonful of some gel she couldn't identify. The mixture looked like a mushy mess. Definitely not powder.

"Missing the last ingredient …" A magnificent boom of

thunder rumbled overhead, shaking the house. "Thunder!" she exclaimed, flipping back through the pages to read snippets. "Nature's Fury … mystical elixir dances with a lightning storm. Harness the potent forces of lightning!"

She shined her light on the worktable again, paying closer attention to things she hadn't really noticed before: pliers, a pair of gloves, a big, oversized spoon, and two electrical wires that were lying across the end of the table. Using her light, she traced the wires off the wooden surface and stretched across the concrete floor. About halfway up the wall, she discovered where the wires ended – or more accurately, where they began. The big switch that looked like a knife reminded her of something out of *Frankenstein*. There were no windows in the underground room, but Jo knew there would be no lightning without thunder. And judging by how quickly and loudly the thunder was booming outside, she figured the lightning show would be spectacular. She'd done her part by putting the lightning rod up on the roof, even though she didn't understand why the journal's author had included it in his drawings. But the lightning rod didn't solve the problem of getting the electric current to hit the bowl with the goop inside—or did it? She made her way back to the table, grabbed the metal bowl, and, using the pliers, attached the end of the wires to each of the metal handles. Another crack of thunder. They were getting closer together.

Jo studied the switch on the wall for a second. She assumed it acted just like a circuit breaker. Now, it was in the down position, which meant off. She held her breath, flipped it up, and quickly stepped back.

Nothing happened. But in the next moment, thunder crashed overhead. The switch on the wall came alive with a flash. Jo jumped back as the current flew down the wires. Blue sparks danced and snaked across the concrete in the dark room, giving the appearance of fireworks on the ground. The current rode the wires up the table and hit the metal bowl. For a moment, the rim of the bowl looked like a small ring of fire. And then it was done—all over in mere seconds.

Jo's heart pounded in her chest. What had just happened? She put the switch on the wall back the way she'd found it and rushed to the table to peer into the bowl. It was filled with a glowing gold powder. The Powder of Life! Jo couldn't believe her own eyes.

She grabbed the bowl but quickly jerked her hand back. The heat radiating from it was intense. She put on the gloves and tried again to pick up the bowl, but it was still too hot. Now, the big spoon made sense. She grabbed it, scooped some powder out of the bowl, and marveled that the powder was still glowing as she carried it into the room that held the characters. She knew just where to start.

Jo stopped in front of Dorothy, her most cherished character from the realm of literature. Snippets of Dorothy's story paraded through Jo's mind. She loved her personality, her ability to daydream, her courage when it came to saving her dog from the wicked witch, and her compassion when she wanted to help the friends she met in Oz.

"Come to life, Dorothy," Jo said softly. "There are so many things we could talk about. We have so much in common. Sometimes, I want to run away from home just like you did. Maybe we could run away together."

Jo held fast to the moment—when there was still a chance of the impossible becoming possible. Finally, she held up the spoon and carefully blew some of the powder across Dorothy's frozen features. Each fine particle settled gently upon her nose and cheeks.

Jo watched anxiously for a sign. Any sign that something was happening. But Dorothy remained motionless as a statue. One minute stretched into two, and Jo's tense shoulders finally slumped in disappointment. "I need you." Her voice trembled. "I need all of you!" She looked down at the glowing powder in the spoon she still held—and in a frenzied state, she rushed along the wax characters, blowing the powder over them as she called out, "Come to life, come to life!" Again and again. When the last of the powder was gone, Jo stood frozen, as still as the characters around her. "Foolish little girl," she scolded herself. The adrenaline and excitement she'd felt just moments ago faded away, leaving her too drained to even cry.

Now, all she wanted was to get out of the enchanted room and out of the basement. Jo lifted the needle from the record, and the room went quiet. She exited and closed the door behind her.

As she crossed the floor back to the worktable, a tremendous crash of thunder startled her. She dropped her flashlight, and it landed on the floor. When she picked it up, the beam hit the ceiling above her. Jo's eyes widened in terror and screamed at the sight above her.

Suspended from a colossal hook attached to the ceiling hung the monstrous gibbet. Inside the iron cage was a gruesome, eerie sight: the skeletal remnants of a human form dressed in a Nazi uniform, bones protruding through the gaps in the cage. Some bones pierced through the bottom, while others jutted out from the sides, creating a grotesque spectacle she could scarcely comprehend. Atop it all, a haunting human skull added a final touch of morbidity. Panicked, her breath whooshed from her lungs, leaving her gasping for air as she lunged towards the stairway. Too late, she realized she had moved too fast, and the room began to spin.

"No, no, no ..."

Dizziness washed over Jo like a tidal wave, blurring her vision and causing her legs to wobble beneath her. The walls warped and contorted, swirling in a disorienting dance around her. Panic swelled within her, threatening to consume her as the spinning room created a tornado of chaos. Jo desperately clung to the hope that she could find her way out before the vertigo swallowed her whole.

"Please, not now," she whispered. Unfortunately, her plea went unanswered as her head struck the concrete floor.

Jo didn't know how long she'd been unconscious when she woke. She groaned and felt her head for any lumps, bumps, or cuts but was happy to discover her latest fall wouldn't result in stitches. Jo sat up and tested her balance by planting her hands on the floor to see if she was still dizzy. But under her palms, something felt hard and scratchy, and she immediately pulled her hands back. She grabbed her flashlight and lit up the floor. The something hard and scratchy was pieces of straw.

Jo got to her feet and gathered her courage to shine her light on the thing that had spooked her.

Since her dad was a history professor and Jo had been his captive student her entire life, she had an in-depth knowledge about the past. She recognized the gibbet hanging from the ceiling from drawings she'd seen. It looked very similar to those used hundreds of years before to publicly execute people. She shivered as she examined the skeleton above her. Whoever the unfortunate soul was that had perished that way had been there long enough to be nothing but bones. Whoever it was had died with a uniform on—a *German officer's* uniform. *A skeleton in the basement of our house. A basement my parents don't know about. Beyond strange and creepy!*

Jo knew it was time to bring her dad up to speed. When she shifted the flashlight off the skeleton there was light in the room that hadn't been there before. Jo looked past the worktable and noticed the door to the enchanted room was open. Jo crossed the huge space and stopped at the threshold.

Jo stared in disbelief at the room where, only minutes ago, dozens of characters had been standing like statues. "It can't be," she whispered. "They're gone."

Chapter 9

A Very Simple Secret

After shutting the door to the enchanted room, Jo hurried upstairs to the wardrobe, where she found more straw and a single brown bean. She left her flashlight on the wardrobe floor and stepped out, eager to find her dad. The thunderstorm that had been pouring rain all morning had subsided, and as she made her way through the quiet house, there were patches of sunlight streaming through the windows.

Normally, she would never consider interrupting one of her dad's Zoom meetings with his students, but there was nothing normal about what had transpired in the basement. She approached the room he called his study and paused to listen at the door. No noise. No dad's voice. She took a chance and knocked lightly. "Dad?" No answer.

Jo opened the door. His computer monitor was dark—the desk chair empty. She hurried back through the house, calling for him as she passed through each room.

Where could he be? He promised to stay home all day and

wouldn't have gone anywhere without leaving a note. *Except I was in the basement that he doesn't even know about. He must have gone to my room, and I wasn't there. He's probably worried!*

She ran to her room, turned off her music, and called her dad. "C'mon, Dad. Pick up." Her call went to voicemail. Frustrated, Jo tried her mom, but she didn't answer either.

Maybe they think I ran away and are looking for me. … Maybe they're worried. … She imagined them searching all over Boston, knocking on doors, calling out, "Jo! Jo March, where are you?!"

Her phone chimed, signaling a new post on TikTok from someone she knew. Jo glanced at the screen where one of her friends from her old school had made a video featuring her dog. However, it was the next video that grabbed her attention. It was the kid from the book club with the Harry Potter glasses, standing next to … Dorothy? Jo's eyes widened in surprise as she turned up the volume on her phone. She quickly hit the replay button to watch the entire video.

"Hey! It's Noah, the ultimate Harry Potter fan, here with Dorothy from Oz! Say hi, Dorothy!" Dorothy gave a little wave, and then Noah panned the camera behind her. "And who do we have here … the rest of the Oz crew …" First there was the Tin Woodman, then the Scarecrow, and just as the camera focused on the Lion … he let out a mighty roar, causing the camera to jerk away as Noah shouted, "Holy Shitaki," and the video cut off abruptly. Glancing at the comments, Jo noticed *#Frostmiddleschool* and realized that was how she'd come across Noah's post.

"They're out there somewhere! Probably scared and wondering where the heck they are. And it's my fault!"

Jo snatched a piece of paper from her desk and scrawled a note to her dad. *If you're wondering where I am, I took an Uber to school.* She paused for a moment, contemplating whether to include the word "love" in her message. She decided against it and signed off simply with "Jo."

Jo ordered an Uber from the app on her phone, issued a quick apology to Nimble about leaving without him, and hurried down the stairs.

As luck would have it, Jo arrived at school during lunch and headed directly to the cafeteria. Ignoring some snarky comments from Carrie and Rose, Jo quickly made her way to the table where the book club kids sat.

Polly greeted her with a big smile. "Jo! I thought you weren't at school today."

"Came late," Jo replied. "Hoping I'd find you guys here."

"Wanna join uth?" Sara asked.

Polly looked at the boys at the table. "Hey, you guys, this is Jo March. The one we told you about."

Jake lifted a hand in greeting. "Hey. I'm Jake. Got math with you."

Jo nodded, then looked at the other boy—the one with the big Harry Potter glasses. He was bent over his phone and grinning. Jake nudged him, and he looked up.

"Oh, hey. I'm Noah," he said.

"Noah the ultimate Harry Potter fan?" Jo asked.

Noah grinned. "Yep."

"I saw your post on TikTok. The one with Dorothy," Jo said.

"You screamed like a girl," Jake giggled.

Noah's eyes widened. "Hey, man, had you been there, you'd have screamed like a girl, too! That lion had giant teeth!"

"Actually, I wanted to ask you about it," Jo said. She sat down at the table. "Where were you when you saw Dorothy?"

"I was heading into Wegmans to grab a bagel for breakfast and there was Dorothy taking straw from the pumpkin display and pretending to stuff the scarecrow's body."

"What did she say?" Jo asked. "How did she seem? Was she confused? Looked lost? What about the others?"

"Geez. Relax. She didn't say anything. At least not that I could hear over my own voice screaming. I'm telling you that lion was real!"

"Yeah, right." Jake chuckled.

"Do you know where they went?"

"No idea."

"Why do you care so much, Jo?" Polly asked.

Jo was already shaking her head as they all turned toward her. "You'd never believe me if I told you."

"Try uth," Sara replied.

"There are more characters running around Boston than just Dorothy and the Oz gang," Jo said.

"How do you know?" Jake asked.

Noah was looking back at the screen on his phone. "Crap, you're right. Someone just posted a video of a guy dressed up like Robin Hood in a tree. It's getting more likes than my Dorothy video."

"Robin Hood? Let me see!" Jo said. Noah held up his phone, and Jo watched Robin Hood fire an arrow from a tree, hitting a squirrel.

"You don't think that was a real squirrel, do you?" Polly asked worriedly.

"I do," Jo said. "And what I'm going to say will sound really crazy ..."

"Go ahead, Jo. No judgment here," Polly said.

Jo hesitated. "I'm responsible for letting Robin Hood,

Dorothy, and many other literary characters out into the world."

The kids stared at her. Jake sighed. "Okay, maybe a little bit of judgment here."

"I get it. You don't know me. And I'm saying something insanely crazy," Jo said. No one argued with her. "But the only reason I'm telling you this is because I need your help finding them."

"Oh, well. Why didn't you say so?" Noah said.

Jo brightened. "Really? You believe me?"

Noah shoved his oversized glasses up on his nose. "No, not really, insanely crazy girl!"

"One in six youths in the U.S. experience a mental health disorder each year. Jo, you could be one of them," Jake said.

"Noah, Jake!" Polly said. "Rude."

"No, they're right. To be honest, I'm not sure I would believe me," Jo admitted. "But let me ask you this: Why would I tell you such a wild story if I couldn't prove to you that it's true?"

"Prove it how?" Sara asked.

Jo looked at the clock on the wall and knew the bell for the class was about to ring. "I can prove it if you'll come home with me after school today."

"Sorry, I'm checking out the Big Top Domain this weekend,"

Jake said. "It opens tonight."

"I saw the commercial for that," Polly said. "I did a Google search and it says the admission price is one book."

"Why a book?" Sara asked. "Ith there thome kind of library inthide that Big Top tent?"

"Who cares why?" Jake said. "It's a cheap admission, and I don't have any money. Spent the last of my birthday money on Minecraft skins."

"So, you're for sure going?" Noah asked.

Jake shrugged. "Why not? The commercial looks unbelievable, and there are some new advances in VR."

"I don't like it," Sara said. "It lookth kind of thcary."

"Scary? It's just VR. Not to mention, the cognitive application is quite impressive. For example, research shows a nine percent improvement in memory accuracy when learning in VR versus looking at a flat-screen TV. It can also be an alternative to prescription drugs for people who have mental disorders. You might want to try it, Jo."

"I agree with Sara," Polly said. "I don't think it's for me."

"Guys! Focus!" Jo yelled, realizing that she didn't just get the attention of the book club but the entire cafeteria. Lowering her voice, Jo continued. "Just give me a chance to prove what I'm saying is true. You can still make it to the Big Top Domain if you don't believe me or want to help."

They hesitated.

"Please? I know it's a lot to ask."

"As long as I text my mom and let her know I'll be late," Polly said. "She'll be fine with it." The others also agreed to go home with her. "Thank you!" Jo said. "I promise this won't be a waste of your time."

Chapter 10
You're Mad, Bonkers

During the three-block walk from the bus stop through the historic neighborhood to Jo's place, the kids passed several houses that had given a serious nod to fall and Halloween. Pumpkins and Jack-o'-lanterns adorned front porches, gauzy white ghosts floated from tree branches, cornstalks surrounded lamp posts, and plastic skeletons danced in the autumn breeze. Since Jo was anxious to get home, her stride was just short of a jog.

"Where's the fire?" Noah sounded a little bit breathless.

Jake, lagging in the back of the group, piped up. "Yeah, Jo. How 'bout slowing the pace a little?"

Jo made the effort to slow down just a bit, but Jake still struggled. "Can't you give us some clue as to what you're going to show us?"

"I think thath fair," Sara said.

"Me too, Jo," Polly said. "I can't wait to see all the wonderful proof."

Jo suddenly stopped on the sidewalk. "You don't have to wait. We're here."

The kids stopped and stared at her house. Jake issued a low whistle at the sight of the broken pickets from the fence, overgrown grass, and weeds, and faded paint that screamed years of neglect. Polly broke their silence.

"Wow," Polly said. "Cool old house."

"Old, yes. But cool?" Noah took off his glasses and offered them to Polly, but she was too busy staring up at the top floor. "Is that an actual widow's walk?"

Jo nodded. "Yes. With an actual lightning rod."

"Hey. You're channeling *Jim Nightshades'* house," Jake said.

Jo smiled at him. "I guess I am."

Noah made a face. "No offense, but this place is a dump."

Sara punched him in the arm. "Noah! Thath's not nice."

"No, he's right," Jo said. "My dad bought it at auction. It needs a ton of work."

"Probably got it pretty cheap," Noah said.

Sara punched him again. "Noah!"

"My dad's a history professor and an aspiring novelist with a great imagination. He sees a ton of potential in it, but my mom's a realtor, and she doesn't see it."

"What do you think, Jo?" Polly asked.

Jo paused for a moment as she stared up at the house. "I think you shouldn't judge a book by its cover."

Jo's nerves were on edge as she led them through the house into the room with the enormous wardrobe.

"This is the big reveal? An old piece of furniture?" Jake asked.

Jo opened the doors of the wardrobe. "We have to go through here and it's going to be dark. I've got one flashlight, but we'll need more."

Sara laughed nervously. "Ith it Narnia?"

Jo looked serious. "Not exactly."

Grabbing their phones, they followed her into the wardrobe, one at a time.

With Jo in the lead, the kids descended the stairs, using the lights from their phones to illuminate each step.

Jo moved farther into the room, but the kids hung back together. She turned and caught them in the flashlight's beam.

Jo was at the long worktable. "C'mon, you guys. I can't show you what I need to show you if you just stay there."

"Kinda like I'd imagine the Potions class at Hogwarts to look,"

Noah observed.

"Any thpiders down here?" Sara asked.

"Spiders? Uh, no spiders," Jo said. "Can you *please* come over here?"

Reluctantly, the kids moved toward her. As they got closer to the worktable, Polly spoke up. "Hey, there's something glowing ..."

Jo nodded and pulled the bowl closer so everyone could peer inside. All eyes were fixed on it, mouths wide open. "What the heck is that stuff?" Jake asked.

"It's called the Powder of Life," Jo replied. "And I made it."

Polly leaned in a bit closer. "Gosh, Jo. All I ever make are brownies. This is amazing."

"You don't even know the half of it," Jo said.

"What's the other half?" Noah asked.

"It's what the powder does. That's the big thing. Well, one of the big things," Jo said. "See this book?"

Jo opened the leather journal on the table. The kids directed their flashlights toward it as she flipped to the drawing of Dorothy. "Look at this!"

Noah leaned in, frowning. "Hey … that looks a lot like the girl in the costume today."

"Look at your TikTok video, Noah," she said. He opened the app and found the video. "Screenshot the part with Dorothy."

After Noah did as she asked, Jo took his phone and placed it next to the drawing of Dorothy. "What do you see?"

"Wow. Two Dorothys," Polly exclaimed.

"Every detail is the same," Jo said. "Her eyes, her braids … her clothes."

"That's so weird! It looks exactly like her," Noah said.

"That's because it *is* her," Jo affirmed. "Remember how you screamed when the Lion roared?"

Noah rolled his eyes. "Thanks for bringing that up."

"Why wouldn't you scream when you were nearly face-to-face with a real lion?"

Noah nodded. "He *did* look real."

She quickly flipped to the drawing of Robin Hood. "Remember the video of the guy who shot the squirrel with an arrow? The one who looked like Robin Hood?" She tapped her finger on the drawing. "This is him."

"Drawings can't leap off the page, Jo," Jake said. "That's logistically impossible."

"True, but drawings can be replicated into life-sized

characters," Jo replied. "Created with wax and other materials along with a lot of the things you see on this very table." She pointed her flashlight at the various fabrics, paints, sheets of tin, human hair, and so on.

Noah chuckled. "Wait. You're trying to tell us that Dorothy and her gang and Robin Hood are …"

"Real," Jo said. "And there's more. Many more characters from classic children's literature."

"Even the thcary onth?" Sara asked.

"There's one … a wolf. But he isn't like the rest," Jo said. "The rest are all heroes of their stories like Snow White, Rapunzel, Mowgli …."

Even as she said it, the skepticism returned to their faces. "I'm not crazy. The author of the journal outlined the whole thing. He sketched the drawings and then used those to create life-sized versions of the characters."

She hurried to the brick wall and shined her flashlight on the knife switch. "Look! The Powder of Life could only be completed with a jolt of electricity. During the thunderstorm this morning, when lightning hit the metal rod on the widow's walk, it traveled down here, and I opened this switch."

Jo swung her light to the concrete floor to highlight the electrical wires. "I watched the current travel from the switch through these wires to the bowl—and it turned to glowing powder."

"The Powder of Life?" Sara asked.

Feeling excited that she was getting through to them, she practically yelled, "Yes!"

Jake had turned back to the journal and was flipping pages when Jo rejoined them at the table. He stopped on the illustrated picture of the man with no name.

"Hey. Who is this guy? Doesn't look like any literary character I know," Jake said.

"The author of the journal wrote that this man was where he poured all his evil thoughts and deeds," Jo explained.

"What is that thaposed to mean?" Sara asked.

Jo sensed that discussing this further could derail her efforts to convince the others about saving the characters. She quickly shifted gears. "I'm not exactly sure, but it's not part of what I'm trying to show you." She tried to turn the page, but Noah's hand blocked her from doing so.

"Wait. I don't know why, but he looks familiar to me."

Polly nodded. "Same here."

"Givths me the heebie-jeebieth," Sara said as a shiver went up her spine.

"Hey, he looks like the guy who owns the Big Top Domain," Jake said. "Except this guy is in some kind of military uniform."

"It's a German uniform," Jo said.

The kids stared at the drawing, taking in all the details.

"I think you're right, Jake," Noah said. The others agreed. "He does look like him. But it's got to be a coincidence, right? What would a drawing of that guy be doing in your secret basement?"

"I haven't figured that out yet," Jo said. "But I have something else to show you." She shined her flashlight on the yellow path on the floor. "Recognize this?"

"Man, whoever dreamed this up really went all out, didn't he? Who has a yellow brick road in their basement?" Jake observed.

"Apparently, Jo does," Noah quipped.

Jo led them along the path to the large wooden door. Jake reached out and traced some of the carved symbols. "The Mines of Moria. Speak, friend, and enter."

"How cool is that?" Noah exclaimed.

The door opened, and the mystical, magical lighting illuminated the space. "Awesome lighting!" Polly said appreciatively. The kids stepped inside and glanced around the empty room.

"This is where all the characters were. Like I said, Dorothy, the other Oz characters, and Robin Hood were just a few of them. After I made the Powder of Life, I decided to try it and see what would happen. See if it was possible to bring inanimate characters to life."

Noah looked incredulous. "Let's recap. You found some guy's journal. You made the Powder of Life, and it worked on the wax characters."

Jo looked relieved enough to cry. "Yes. That's exactly what I'm telling you."

"So … you actually saw them all come to life?" Jake asked.

Jo hesitated. "Not exactly. I have something called Meniere's Disease. Sometimes, if I move too fast, I lose my balance. That's what happened right after I used the powder on the characters. I fell and knocked myself out. When I came to, they were all gone."

Jake sighed. "I think you just explained the whole thing in a nutshell, Jo. While you were unconscious, you had a series of dreams. It's not uncommon for people to experience sci-fi-like episodes or have paranoid delusions while they're in that altered state."

"That's not what happened to me, Jake," she insisted. "If all of this is just a paranoid delusion, then how do you explain Noah meeting Dorothy on the street? Why is Robin Hood running around the city shooting squirrels? What about the journal or the Powder of Life?"

Jake shrugged. "I can't explain the weird coincidences you just mentioned. But I'm sticking with my theory. It was your subconscious while you were out cold."

As he walked away from the enchanted room, Jo turned to the others. "Please believe me. This wasn't a dream …"

She was interrupted by a very loud scream, followed by a bewildered "What the heck?"

The kids turned to see Jake's flashlight shining on the ceiling, specifically illuminating the skeletal remains inside the iron cage.

Polly and Sara both screamed and hid behind Noah.

"Holy smokes, Jo," Jake said. "Is this your idea of a Halloween prank?"

"No prank. He's real. Or he was real," Jo said.

One by one, the kids moved closer to illuminate the gruesome scene with their own flashlights. Jo stepped closer to look up at the iron cage. "That cage is called a gibbet. They used it in medieval times to publicly execute people. It hung from gallows or trees or anything they could find. I guess they thought if people watched someone die an agonizing death, it would keep them in line."

"How do you know all that?" Noah asked.

"Remember, my dad's a history professor," Jo answered. "I grew up learning about stuff like that."

"Thath tho groth." Sara shuddered.

Jake hadn't taken his eyes off the bones in the gibbet. "You know the FBI solved only fifty-four percent of murder cases last year.

Any idea who that was?"

"My guess is he's the author of the journal and the creator of all the characters," Jo said. "And I'm thinking the no-name guy killed him."

"And your parents are fine with all this R.L. Stine stuff in your basement?" Jake asked.

"I haven't had a chance to tell them yet," Jo said evasively.

Polly couldn't bear to look at the gruesome sight any longer. "That's enough for me. I'm out."

Sara nodded. "Same here. Sorry, Jo. It's all too weird and creepy."

"Look, you guys, I know this all sounds crazy, but I swear I'm telling the truth. It's my fault that all the characters are loose in a world they don't understand. I'd never forgive myself if something happened to them. And I can't find them all by myself. I need your help."

Noah shook his head. "It's all too much. No hard feelings, though, okay?"

"Fine. I guess I'll just have to find them on my own," Jo said, trying to evoke guilt, but no one seemed affected.

As they climbed the stairs, Jake chimed in. "Hey, look on the bright side, Jo."

"What bright side?"

"You'll definitely have the best Halloween decorations on the block if you hang that gibbet thing from a tree in your front yard."

Chapter 11

Still Like Dust, I Rise

Jo opened the front door for her classmates. "Sorry for wasting your time, guys, and … sharing just how bonkers I am."

"We don't think you're bonkers," Polly said. "You just have some crazy ideas and strange stuff in your basement."

Sara put a hand on Jo's shoulder. "We'll thee you Monday at thchool. You're a valuable new member of the book club."

"You've got our numbers now," Polly said. "Text or call me anytime. Except after nine on school nights."

Jo watched as the kids made their way down the sidewalk, lit by the twilight sky.

Now what? Dorothy and the characters are still in danger and the only kids who could have helped me think I'm just the crazy new girl who believes in a world of faith and trust and pixie dust.

She let out a disappointed sigh and shut the door. As Jo made her way up the stairs to her room, a knock on the door made her quickly retrace her steps. She opened the door with a smile. "Change your minds..."

But the smile dropped when she came face to face with the no-name man from the leather journal. Instead of a German uniform, he wore a gray, double-breasted jacket, a white shirt, a black tie, and trousers. Even his shoes were shiny black. Jo looked into his flat, black eyes and took a step back. The no-name man conjured up a strained smile.

"Good afternoon. My name is Silas Schutzstaffel," he said. "And you are?"

Jo almost didn't believe her own eyes. The man, filled with evil, prideful thoughts, was standing at her front door. She answered him without even thinking. "Joanna March."

"Ah, Miss March, is the man or woman of the house at home?"

Jo looked past Silas at a black, ornate Mercedes-Benz Tourenwagen parked in the street in front of her house. Standing beside the car was a small man, barely five feet tall. He stared at her, then slicked his shaggy, oily hair back with one hand. Prickles of fear ran up her spine as she looked from the creepy man back to Silas. Reaching into her back pocket for her phone, she glanced at the screen. She tapped out something on the keyboard.

"Miss March?" Silas said impatiently.

"I'm sorry," she said. "What was the question?"

"Your parents … are they home?" he asked.

She answered quickly. "Yes."

Silas studied her for a moment. "May I speak to one of them, please?"

"They're too busy to come to the door right now," Jo said. "Can I give them a message?"

"There's no reason to bother them," Silas said. "If you'll be so kind as to help me, I can collect what I came for and be on my way."

"Collect what?" Jo knew her voice sounded strained. Silas made her very uneasy.

"I was a previous resident of this lovely home, and when I moved, I left something behind. I want to get it back," he said.

"When did you live here?" Jo asked.

Silas forced another smile that looked more like a grimace. "It's been quite a while. But I believe what I came for is still here."

Jo looked skeptical. "Maybe, but I doubt it. What did you leave behind?"

"I'm afraid that's personal," Silas said.

"And I'm afraid I can't help you." She started to close the door, but Silas quickly stiff-armed it to prevent her from shutting it. Jo's heartbeat quickened.

"Let me appeal to you one more time," he said. "I'm only in town for a few days. Maybe you've seen my ads online or on TV? I'm the owner and proprietor of the Big Top Domain."

"I've seen them," Jo said. "Lots of kids at school are talking about it."

Silas looked pleased. "Wonderful! I'm so happy to hear it. This will be our inaugural event. I'm calling it *Triumph of the Will*."

Jo's brows shot up. "How interesting to name it after a film."

Silas frowned. "And even more interesting, someone your age has heard of it."

Jo didn't respond but tried to close the door again. Silas kept his arm in place, bony fingers splayed on the faded wood. "In any event, we are very excited to have the youth of Boston come and experience what we offer."

"Whoever has the youth has the future," Jo whispered. Silas stared at her, then offered another forced smile.

"Well, the plot thickens. She quotes *Mein Kamf*. A history buff and a book lover. Not many children have read a book by Hitler." Silas's German accent grew even more pronounced as he spoke. When Jo didn't respond, he continued. "Shouldn't you be reading more age-appropriate books, such as children's classics?"

Worried about what was coming next, Jo swallowed hard but

nodded. "I've read those too."

"No doubt you've seen the postings and videos of some very famous literary characters that have been spotted in and around the city?" he asked.

"I've seen a few," she admitted, even while her stomach clenched in a knot of nerves.

Silas tilted his head and studied her. "Why do you suppose this is happening?"

"I'm not sure," Jo said. "Maybe it's the Boston Public Library trying to get kids interested in books again."

Silas shook his head. "I think we both know better than that, don't we?"

The knot in Jo's stomach tightened. "What do you mean?"

"If the library were trying to distract children from the games that consume them and get them interested in books again, they would use superheroes around town. Graphic novel heroes. Certainly not some girl in a blue-and-white gingham dress with braids."

Jo knew he was baiting her, but she couldn't help herself. "Everyone knows who Dorothy Gale is! She's one of the most iconic characters in classic literature!"

"Maybe decades ago," Silas said, "but now I'll bet not even one in five children would recognize her. And that goes for the rest of those ancient characters. They are all has-beens. Children today are too sophisticated for those silly stories."

"They are not silly," she said, "and anyone who has read those classic stories will always cherish those characters."

Silas offered a tolerant smile. "I'm thinking I may just round them up..."

"And do what?" Jo practically shouted.

"Let's quit playing games, Miss March. I believe you know why I'm here and what I want. You used the Powder of Life on those characters! You're the reason they're running all over Boston."

"You know nothing." Jo hoped she sounded braver than she felt. "And you're trespassing. You need to leave before I call the police."

"Give me the Powder of Life. It's rightfully mine, and I intend to get it one way or another," Silas said.

"I don't have it," she said.

"You're lying," Silas scolded. Stepping closer, he pushed against the door. "Beware; for I am fearless and, therefore, powerful." A hot stab of terror pierced her when she realized Silas was determined to enter the house. Panic bubbled up inside, but before she could vocalize her fear, a voice called out.

"Jo!"

Silas heard it, too, and he turned to see Polly, Sara, Jake, and Noah coming up the sidewalk toward the house. Jo nearly fainted with relief.

Silas withdrew his hand from the door but leaned menacingly towards Jo. "Remember this, Jo March, our conflict is far from concluded. You have a mere twenty-four hours to give me the Powder of Life, or else I shall track down every single one of your literary companions and eradicate them systematically and without mercy."

Silas turned and strode down the sidewalk, brushing past the kids, who stared as he approached his car and driver. The driver opened the back door of the Mercedes. "We done here, boss?"

"We're just getting started, Ezra." Silas climbed into the car, and Ezra hurried to get behind the wheel. As they drove away, Jo ran down the sidewalk.

"I got your text, Jo! We figured SOS meant you wanted us to come back," Polly said.

"I've never been so happy to see anyone in my life!" Jo exclaimed.

Noah looked after the car, then at Jo. "I know this is going to sound crazy, but that guy looks exactly like the one in the drawing we saw."

Jo nodded. "His name is Silas, and he owns the Big Top Domain."

"Why was he here? And why was he yelling at you?" Jake asked.

"He came for the Powder of Life," Jo said. "He's seen the characters around town and knew someone used it on them. And now he knows it was me."

"Why would he want it?" Polly asked.

Jo shook her head. "I don't know, but he told me he would 'eradicate' all the characters if I don't give it to him within twenty-four hours."

"That doesn't give us much time! We can't let him destroy the characters," Polly said.

"Then you believe me?" Jo asked.

"It seems impossible," Polly said, "but after seeing that mean man here and knowing he's one of the drawings in that journal ... and he's threatening you and the characters ..."

"Geez, Polly, just say yes! Yes, we believe you now, Jo," Jake said.

Jo looked visibly relieved. "Thanks, guys! You have no idea how much that means to me."

"Shouldn't you just give him the Powder of Life, Jo?" Noah said.

"No, I won't," Jo said. "If it can bring wax figures to life, what else could it do? Just imagine what a man like Silas would do with it."

"Tho now what?" Sara asked.

"I'm going to need help finding them," Jo said. "I can't do it alone."

Noah chimed in. "Well, you can't stay in your corner of the forest waiting for others to come to you. You have to go to them sometimes."

"Who said that?" Jake asked.

Noah replied, "Winnie the Pooh."

"How in the world are we going to find all the characters in a city the thize of Bothton?" Sara asked.

"We need to follow whatever clues we can find," Jo said.

"Like a scavenger hunt?" Polly asked.

"Yeah, kind of like a scavenger hunt," Jo said. "We absolutely can't let Silas find and destroy them."

"I know the clock is ticking, Jo," Noah said, "but the sun is going down, and if I don't get home soon, I'll be grounded and spend tomorrow and Sunday in my room. I'll be no help at all."

Everyone agreed. First thing in the morning, they'd hit the streets of Boston and find the characters before Silas could get his hands on them and make good on his evil promise.

Chapter 12
A Wild Thing

After a strategy meeting that morning, Jo and the book club kids decided the best places in the city were all part of what Bostonians called "The Emerald Necklace."

It was a network of nine sections linked by parkways and waterways, each with its own distinct features: a bustling downtown park, a shopping mall park, an arboretum, and the list went on. It felt like a place that literary characters might be drawn to in order to explore their stories. Splitting up seemed like the best way to cover more ground. Jake said he'd take Franklin Park; a place he'd been going to with his parents for years. Polly was going to search at the mall, while Noah and Sara took different sections of the city on foot. They promised to text or call Jo if they stumbled upon any of the characters.

Jo left her dad a note on the counter next to the coffeemaker, letting him know she was hanging out with her new book club friends. Not *exactly* a lie. She rushed out of the house, glancing at her watch, and realized she'd barely make it to the bus stop in time for the next departure. Jo adjusted the lanyard around her neck; her mom's water-resistant passport pouch had seemed like the perfect hiding place for the Powder of Life. She could wear it under her clothes for safekeeping, and no one would be the wiser.

Knowing she would be cutting it close, Jo decided to leave the footpath canopied by trees and cut across the grass. That was when she saw it--a cluster of black tents forming a circle around a larger, grand tent. A flag proudly fluttered atop the impressive big top, boldly declaring its name: Big Top Domain. Jo watched as kids of various ages streamed eagerly toward the entrance. So captivated by the unique spectacle, she nearly walked right into the path of a boy on a bike. The boy slammed on his brakes, narrowly avoiding Jo with his front tire.

"Wow! Nice move, new girl!" He sounded both surprised and concerned. "Didn't you see me?"

Startled, Jo looked into the face of the cute blond boy from the cafeteria. "No, I'm sorry. I wasn't looking where I was going."

"That's twice I've saved you," he said with a grin. "I'm Drew, by the way."

"I'm Jo," she said. "Sorry again. For having to save me twice."

"No worries. So, are you headed to the Big Top Domain?" he asked.

She shook her head. "No. I'm in a hurry. Every minute that passes means they're in danger."

"Who are you talking about?"

"No time to explain," she said. "I gotta catch the bus." She continued on her way.

Confused, Drew called after her, "What danger?"

Jo called back over her shoulder, "I need to save the characters."

"What characters?"

But she simply waved her hand dismissively and kept walking quickly to the other side of the park.

Drew shook his head. "Strange girl." And just as he was about to pedal away, a sharp pain in the back of his head stopped him. "Ouch!" he exclaimed, noticing a rock near the back tire of his bike. He scanned the area for any sign of the culprit but found no one. However, when he turned back around, his eyes widened in astonishment. Standing before him was a man dressed entirely in green: a green tunic, green pants, green shoes, and a green hat. Strapped across his back was a quiver filled with arrows, and he stood with his hands confidently placed on his hips.

Unfazed by Drew's surprise, the green-clad man announced, "I'm afraid I must commandeer your tiny chariot."

Jo heaved a sigh of relief as she took a seat in the middle of the city bus. She kept her eyes peeled out the window for anything or anyone unusual. Only five minutes into her ride, her phone vibrated with a FaceTime call from Noah. His face filled her screen, his eyes wide behind the lenses of his round glasses.

"Yo! You're not going to believe this," he said in a hushed voice. "Check this out!" Noah shifted his camera to frame a man sitting on the other end of a park bench—wearing nothing but his birthday suit—reading a newspaper. Noah's face filled the screen again. "Trust me when I tell you the only thing this guy is wearing is a grim expression. He must be the emperor with no clothes! What do I do? I can't just grab a naked man."

Jo shook her head. "Eww. Do *not* grab him! There was no naked emperor among the characters."

Noah let out a huge sigh of relief. "Thank you, God. I'd rather grab Lord Voldemort than touch this guy. See ya."

As soon as Noah's call ended, Jo received a text from Jake. ***Pretty sure I just saw the Reluctant Dragon in Franklin Park Zoo.*** Moments later, another message from Jake arrived—this one a video. Jo watched as he panned across the sculpture of the ice-breathing dragon that the zoo displayed every year. Then he zoomed in on a blue dragon with a shiny green tail, curled up on the grass, asleep beneath the ice dragon. Children scrambled up the back of the blue dragon, causing it to ripple under their weight. Startled, the kids fell off, and the blue dragon got to his feet—and flew away. Jo quickly replied: ***Follow that dragon!***

Just as Jo pressed send on her text to Jake, her phone rang. "Jo! It's Polly. Hey, I got sidetracked … this poor little boy is lost, and I'm helping him find his mom. What's that? Oh, sweetie, you can't use those to buy anything. Here, just toss them in the planter." Jo listened patiently for Polly to finish. "Sorry, Jo … the cute little boy thought he could buy food with some beans."

Jo quickly interjected, "Beans? Ask him what kind of beans!"

"Sweetie, what kind of beans were they? Pinto, black, kidney?"

Jo strained to hear the boy's answer.

"Magic beans?" Polly repeated. Suddenly, a realization dawned on her. "Wait a minute," Polly said. "Did you say *magic* beans?"

Jo practically shouted, "That's Jack!"

The bus driver stopped along the route and opened the door, and several people made their way to exit. Jo's phone pinged. Another message, this one a photo. It was of Sara standing in front of a boutique window, taking what appeared to be a selfie. Upon closer inspection, Sara was pointing to the window, where a boy stood as rigid as a statue. A boy who almost looked like he could be made of wood. A boy with a very, very long nose.

"Oh my gosh, she's found Pinocchio!" Jo said.

Although Jo felt some relief about the characters that had been discovered, her concern for Dorothy lingered. Where would she go?

The obvious answer was the Emerald City to see the Great and Powerful Oz. But there was no way she would find that in Boston. Jo turned her gaze back to the window to spot anything out of the ordinary.

Then, suddenly, the *out-of-the-ordinary* caught her attention as the bus came to a halt at the intersection of Tremont and Clarendon Streets. The area was buzzing with activity, filled with curious onlookers, frustrated drivers honking their horns, and the distant wail of sirens from emergency vehicles. The other passengers on the bus leaned forward, straining to see what was causing the commotion. Rising from her seat, Jo joined the other curious riders peering outside the window.

Chapter 13

We Live in a Rainbow of Chaos

It was a chaotic scene. In the center of the intersection, a Boston Police officer took charge, wielding a bullhorn as he directed the crowd. He urged everyone to return to their vehicles or find shelter in the nearest building. People quickly did as they were instructed. Inside the bus, passengers speculated between themselves about the cause of the disturbance. A range of theories was suggested, with some attributing it to acts of terrorism, while others feared a potentially hazardous chemical spill.

Jo dismissed the theories as quickly as she heard them. She had her own idea about what was happening on the street.

"Folks, folks! I've got some information you'll want to hear, so if you'd pipe down a minute ..." the bus driver said. The restless chatter among the passengers quieted, and he continued. "I just heard from my dispatcher that, believe it or not, there is an angry lion on the loose. We will sit tight until the authorities contain the threat."

I'll bet he's not a threat. I'll bet he's the Lion I'm looking for ... and that means Dorothy, Scarecrow, and Tin Woodman must be close. He's scared of his own shadow, so he must be terrified.

Jo needed to reach the Lion quickly to find Dorothy and the others before something bad happened. She hurried up the aisle to the bus driver.

"I need to get off right now."

He shook his head. "No way, not happening, little lady."

"Please, just open the door," she said.

"Didn't you hear what I just said? There is a lion on the loose."

As the bus driver rambled on about safety, Jo's mind raced for a solution. *"Make sure everything you do is so completely crazy, it's unbelievable."* *Okay*, she thought. *Crazy, here I come!*

Jo looked out the window, past the driver, and pointed to a car. "That's my mom. Please! I'm scared! I just want to be with her!"

The bus driver, raising an eyebrow in skepticism, cracked open his side window to call out to the woman in the car. Seizing the moment, Jo hit the button controlling the doors and leaped off the bus.

Even though the bus driver kept yelling for her to return, Jo ignored him, determined to find her way through the maze of stopped cars. Periodically, she jumped up and down, but her frustration mounted with every attempt. *I need to be higher so I can see what's happening.*

Without pausing to consider the consequences, she climbed onto the rear bumper of a silver Ford and planted her sneakers firmly on the back windshield to shimmy up to the roof. In the back of her mind, she registered the driver's protests, but determined to get to the top of the car, she pressed on.

As Jo stood atop the roof, her gaze was instantly captivated by the spot teeming with activity. Her breath caught in her throat as she spotted the "ferocious lion" that had caused the tangled mess of traffic and panic. *It's him. It's really him.* The beloved Lion from The Wonderful Wizard of Oz was snarling and growling at the two policemen who had their handguns drawn. Jo knew the lion would never intentionally hurt anyone, and his reactions were driven by fear, not malice.

Dorothy would never abandon the lion. She has to be close. Jo quickly scanned the area around the lion. *There!* Several yards away, huddled together watching their friend, stood Tin Woodman, Scarecrow, and … Dorothy, clutching the basket with Toto inside. Suddenly, Jo's eyes filled with tears as she stood transfixed at the sight of her favorite character from literature. *Why am I crying?* she thought as a smile spread across her face.

"Hey! You!" a woman in the car shouted. "Get off the roof of my car this instant!"

Jo peeked over the roof of the car at Miss Windsor, the school lunch monitor, who had her head sticking out the window, her jaw dropped in disbelief. "Joanna March?"

Jo was just as shocked that out of all the cars at the intersection, she had picked this one to climb onto. *What are the odds? Not even Jake would know.*

Miss Windsor scowled at her. "As if it wasn't enough that you turned my spotless cafeteria into a complete mess, now you're denting the roof of my car! Get down this instant!"

Jo yelled down to Miss Windsor, "I don't want to ruin an apology with an excuse but trust me, I've got a good one!" She shifted her focus back to the unfolding chaos, which now included a police officer in a Chevy Tahoe, braking on the sidewalk a few yards away. As he opened the tailgate to grab his equipment, he spotted Jo and strode toward her.

"Hey! Get down from there!"

Miss Windsor was pounding on her car door, still yelling for Jo to get down. So she did. Jo dropped to her butt, slid down the windshield, and hopped off the hood as the officer grabbed her arm.

What's my plan? Miss Windsor was practically babbling inside the car. *She actually sounds like she's in distress.*

Jo pointed at Miss Windsor. "Help! My mom is having a heart attack!"

Reacting swiftly, the officer turned his attention towards Miss Windsor. Jo took a second to gauge the distance to the lion. She could easily cover that ground. *But once there, how will I get them to safety?*

Jo spotted the police Tahoe idling just a few feet away. *No guts, no glory, Jo!* As the officer was trying to calm Miss Windsor down she took the opportunity to race to the Tahoe and jump into the driver's seat. But then she froze. The only time she had ever driven a car was when she sat on her dad's lap as a little girl while he let her steer in the mall parking lot. Her mind raced through the necessary steps: *gas pedal on the right, brake on the left.* She stomped on the gas; the engine revved, but the vehicle didn't move. *Hurry, hurry, hurry!* She looked frantically at the gauges, buttons, and numbers on the dashboard display.

A sudden rap on the driver's window startled her. "What do you think you're doing?" the officer growled. "Out! Now!" In that moment, Jo remembered what step she'd missed. *D for Drive! Put it in D!* She hit the gas pedal again, and the Tahoe shot forward like a rocket. Her head snapped back against the headrest, and from the corner of her eye, saw the officer jump back from the vehicle. Fumbling for a second, she found the switch for the siren and flipped it on.

As the blaring siren reverberated through the air, it caught the attention of the two officers who had the lion cornered. They swiftly pivoted their attention to the Tahoe hurtling toward them. The officers instinctively scattered, giving Jo an opening. She jerked the steering wheel to the right and then slammed on the brakes, causing the vehicle to skid sideways. It came to an abrupt stop between the Lion and the Oz crew. Jo pressed the button to lower the passenger window.

"Get in! I'm a friend, and I'll take you away from here!"

Dorothy hesitated, and Jo yelled out the back, "Please, Lion! Don't be afraid. I just want to help!"

Desperate to escape, the Lion leaped through the open tailgate; his friends Dorothy and Toto, Scarecrow, and Tin Woodman climbed in as well. The police officers shouted at Jo to get out of the car and run! But caught in the whirlwind of chaos, Jo barely had a moment to grasp the incredible sight of her beloved characters finding refuge in the car. And there, draped over the backseat with sheer joy, was the Lion, thrilled to be reunited with his friends. *Oh my gosh … this is really happening! Now what? Get them to safety …*

"Hang on!" Jo shouted. "New driver here."

Jo stomped on the accelerator, causing the SUV to lurch forward aggressively. Gripping the steering wheel with white-knuckled grit, she careened down the sidewalk, blaring the horn to warn pedestrians to get out of her way. The outdoor tables, abandoned by diners just moments before, splintered into pieces as the vehicle crashed through them.

Then, out of nowhere, a mother pushing a baby stroller emerged from a store directly in the SUV's path.

Oh no, no, no, no … Jo panicked and swerved to avoid them, narrowly missing a catastrophic collision. But the SUV careened into a nearby fire hydrant. In an instant, the airbags deployed with a deafening pop, striking Jo and Dorothy in the face.

Dazed and confused, Jo struggled to make sense of the pandemonium around her. Slowly, she turned to the Oz characters, who looked both concerned and bewildered.

"Everyone okay?" Jo asked.

"Is this what you call being helpful?" asked the Scarecrow. "Because right now it seems we're in bigger trouble than we were."

"My name is Jo March, and I promise I'm trying to help," Jo said.

"Look!" Dorothy exclaimed, pointing out the windshield. Diffused sunlight filtered through the mist from the geyser of the hydrant, creating a beautiful rainbow arching over the tallest building in Boston. "Is that the Emerald City?"

Jo followed Dorothy's gaze, realizing she was pointing at what she knew as the Hancock Building on Clarendon Street. The skyscraper's blue glass walls reflected the sky and everything around it.

"Emerald City?" Jo asked.

Dorothy nodded. "Yes. I know my house landed in Oz, but we are trying desperately to get to the Emerald City to see the Great and Powerful Wizard."

Oh my gosh. Dorothy knows her own story. Does that mean she knows what happens in the end? Or does she only know details as they unfold …?

"We need to get out of here, quickly," Jo said. "Those people running toward us want to stop you from getting to the Emerald City."

"But the Good Witch of the North gave me a kiss on my forehead for protection," Dorothy said.

"I'm sure that's true, but right now I don't think that's enough. You all need to come with me," Jo said.

"How do we know we can trust you?" the Tin Woodman asked.

"Um … I know Glinda, the Good Witch of the South," Jo said. "She sent word from her castle in Quadling Country for me to do all I can to see that you get what you need to go home."

"Home!? Do you hear that, Toto? She'll help us get home!" Dorothy said. "We're ready to go with you, Jo. Lead the way!"

Jo looked at the officers who were heading straight toward them. *We'll never be able to outrun them. Unless …*

"How would you feel about giving us a ride, Lion?" Jo asked. "I know you can run faster than any of us."

The Lion looked pleased at the compliment. "Lions run fast and leap far. I'm not sure if you will all fit on my back, but we can try."

The Lion lowered himself to the ground so Dorothy and Jo could climb on. The Scarecrow tucked himself between Jo and the tail end of the Lion. Jo looked at the Tin Woodman.

"Can you grab Lion's tail and hang on?"

"I have a steel grip!" Tin Woodman said.

And with that, Lion took off, bounding away from the approaching police officers. Tin Woodman flew along behind them, bouncing off the concrete every few feet and causing sparks to fly. Jo, her hand caught up in Lion's mane, grinned despite their predicament. Never in her wildest imagination had she ever thought she'd be racing along the streets of Boston on the back of the Cowardly Lion from Oz. Now, she needed to get Dorothy and her friends someplace safe. Autumn days grew shorter, and darkness would come quickly. There was no way she was going to make it home before they ran out of daylight.

Chapter 14

I Can Feel Little Invisible Strings

Silas paced in the dimly lit living room, listening to the footsteps on the second floor. The creaks groans, and squeaks of aged wood told the story of where someone might be. Impatient, he finally went to stand at the base of the staircase. Moments later, a flashlight beam broke through the darkness as Ezra hurried down the stairs. "I checked every room. No one's here. Not even the girl."

Silas frowned as he contemplated his next move. After a brief pause, he knew what to do. "Come with me," he instructed, his voice low but determined.

Silas and Ezra descended the stairs into the dark expanse of the basement. Silas snatched the flashlight from Ezra's grip. "Give it here." Using the glow of light, Silas scoured the laboratory equipment on the worktable, his eyes burning with desire. The light's cone shape settled upon the metal bowl. He quickly slid it towards him, only to find it empty. Like a bottomless pit of secrets, his expression grew even darker.

"Where. Is. It?"

The chilling tone sent shivers down Ezra's spine. "I'm sure it's here somewhere." Ezra's voice quivered.

Silas moved the light over the table again. "She took it. And the book is gone, too. That meddling girl!"

"Book?" Ezra parroted.

Silas looked thoughtful. "It contains the instructions on how to make the Powder of Life."

With a swift motion, Silas turned, casting the light across the empty space. The deep darkness seemed to swallow their hopes, leaving only remnants of Silas' twisted past. "This place, once my home, witnessed the rebirth of my existence." His voice was bittersweet.

Silas swung the beam of light towards the gibbet dangling from the ceiling, revealing the haunting sight of the skeletal remains. Silas couldn't help but feel delight in the presence of such macabre decay.

Curious, Ezra pointed at it. "Someone you knew, boss?"

Silas shook his head, his expression solemn. "Only for a brief moment. That was my maker."

Ezra looked from the skeleton back to Silas. "Seems like someone betrayed him."

Silas looked back at the gibbet. "For there to be betrayal, there would have to have been trust first."

Nervously, Ezra tapped his fingers against the worn, wooden surface of the worktable. "So, what now?"

Deep in thought, Silas's gaze drifted over the bench. "These silly characters running around Boston are a distraction, pulling attention away from the Big Top Domain. We need to put an end to it."

Ezra absentmindedly scratched at his oily hair. "I don't understand, boss. If you knew the makings for the Powder of Life were here, why didn't you come back sooner?"

"I did come back," Silas said. "I came back and waited for the perfect electrical storm that would turn the simple ingredients into the Powder of Life. I waited and waited. And waited some more, but the storm never materialized."

"Couldn't you have made it without an electrical storm?" Ezra questioned.

Silas shook his head. "Lightning reaches temperatures around 54,000 Fahrenheit, which is five times hotter than the surface of the sun. It's the only way to turn the ingredients into the Powder of Life."

"So now we just need to wait for that girl to come back, right, boss?"

"No, fool," Silas said. His determination was evident in his voice. "She will come to us."

Ezra sighed, and his shoulders slumped in defeat. "But that's impossible. There's no way she'd come anywhere near us."

Silas swiftly corrected him, his tone unwavering. "We don't entertain the notion of 'impossible,' Ezra!"

Once again, Silas surveyed the room, finally seeing something that brought a smile to his face.

"When all else fails, follow the yellow brick road."

"I don't get it," Ezra said. He fell into step behind Silas, and they both followed the yellow path on the floor to the enchanted room.

Pausing at the doorway, Silas savored the moment. "Finally, I can step inside."

Ezra looked up at him, puzzled. "What's the story here?"

Silas still didn't move. "I was not allowed into this inner sanctum."

"We going in or what?" Ezra said impatiently.

Silas nodded and slowly stepped over the threshold of the door. Instantly, the motion activated the soft, enchanting glow.

Ezra looked around at the nearly empty room and stated the obvious. "So, what we got here is a chair, a table with a gadget, and a whole lot of nothing else."

Silas moved toward the chair and took a seat. "It's the whole lot of nothing else that we need to talk about, Ezra. They were here. All the literary characters the March girl unleashed on the city were in this room. Kept separate from me so I wouldn't taint their precious purity."

Silas turned to look at the old phonograph on the table beside him. He turned the crank and carefully placed the needle on the vinyl record. The tune of Swan Lake filled the room.

Caught up in the moment, Silas hummed along with it, completely lost in the enchanting notes. It took Ezra calling out to him to break his trance-like state.

"Umm, boss? Yo ... boss!"

Silas snapped back to reality and opened his eyes, shaking off the euphoria.

"We still need a plan to get the kid to bring us the Powder of Life."

In the next moment, Silas connected the dots. He smiled.

"She's one little girl, and we know what, or rather who, she's after. All we need to do is round up those characters and use them as bait for Miss March. Being the heroine she is, she won't be able to resist coming to save them."

"Not to sound like a broken record, boss, but we still don't have a plan to round up dozens of characters," Ezra said.

Silas smiled. "Ah, yes, we do, Ezra. And music is part of it."

Silas removed the needle and carefully picked up the phonograph, clasping it in his hands. His eyes were shining with determination and confidence. "It's the perfect plan."

Chapter 15
You Have Been My Friend

The abandoned warehouse stood amidst other old, dilapidated buildings. The windows, now shattered or boarded up, allowed only feeble moonlight to penetrate the darkness within. A sense of eerie stillness hung in the air. The vast space was filled with remnants of what once was—a labyrinth of office rooms and machinery.

Fast asleep on the worn-out floor, the Lion lay curled up around Toto, with Scarecrow and Tin Woodman using him as a pillow. Jo and Dorothy sat nearby, heads together, watching the news on Jo's phone. The first segment was of the gorilla habitat at the Franklin Zoo. The reporter stood in front of the glass window while several gorillas milled around in the enclosure behind her.

"I'm at the Gorilla Habitat at the Franklin Zoo, where earlier today, people here almost witnessed a tragedy. A zoo patron happened to catch this amazing scene." While Jo and Dorothy watched, the video changed to a large group of people admiring the gorillas. The adults were lost in conversation while a three-year-old boy managed to climb up the fence and drop into the gorilla's enclosure. People in the crowd started to scream; the loudest among them were the parents of the little boy. While they watched in horror, a giant three-hundred-pound Silverback charged toward the little boy. The boy's father tried to get a foothold on the fence of the enclosure, but before he could even start to climb, a slight boy with shaggy black hair came out of nowhere, swooping across the habitat by one of the ropes hanging from the roof.

"Look!" someone yelled, pointing at the boy, who wore nothing but a loincloth. The crowd gasped at the boy's foolhardy bravery. Jo gasped but for a different reason. "That's Mowgli!" she exclaimed.

Mowgli dropped from the rope and swiftly grabbed the three-year-old before the Silverback could react. Swinging the child onto his back, Mowgli scaled the rock wall that led to the same fence he had climbed. Upon reaching the top, he was met by the boy's grateful father, who eagerly grabbed his son. The crowd erupted in cheers, but Mowgli was already back on the habitat floor. The angry gorillas tried to confront him, but he scurried across the ground on all fours, reached the rock wall on the opposite side, and, in the blink of an eye, scaled it and disappeared from view.

The reporter reappeared on the screen. "A tragedy averted thanks to one very brave boy. We don't yet know his identity but would love any information from the public who might recognize him. In other news, this next video surfaced earlier."

Now on Jo's phone, a grainy security recording unfolded,

revealing Noah and Aladdin sitting on top of a large pile of oriental rugs in the center of a store.

Amidst the owner's conversation with an elderly couple, his gaze momentarily shifted towards the mischievous duo, urging them to get off the valuable merchandise. But instead of complying, Aladdin grabbed the edge of the rug, and Noah quickly followed suit. The owner strode toward them but stopped in disbelief as the rug lifted into the air, defying gravity and leaving the owner frozen in astonishment. Meanwhile, the older couple fled for safety, flinging open the door, and instinctively ducked just as the levitating carpet sailed above their heads and vanished into the outside world.

The reporter appeared again. "And this extraordinary event took place today at the mall." The camera zoomed out to reveal a gigantic tree-like trunk stretching through the roof. "As you can clearly see, what can only be described as a beanstalk has burst through the ceiling. The spectacle is truly amazing and has drawn quite a crowd." The reporter approached a teen boy among the onlookers and thrust her microphone at him. "What are your thoughts right now for our viewers at home?" The teen beamed with excitement. "This is the coolest thing I've ever seen! I was planning on going to the Big Top Domain today, but that's just virtual reality. This right here is real-world stuff. I'm hanging out to see if a giant comes down that beanstalk!"

The reporter stepped away from the teenager. "At this time,

no officials have dared to scale the beanstalk to determine its height. And in keeping with our theme of odd events, there was this." The image on Jo's phone changed to Slugworth's Candy Shop.

"This afternoon, in the heart of the city, the largest candy heist ever witnessed took place. Fortunately, some quick-thinking customers captured the entire incident on video." Jake appeared on screen, using a rope made of Nerds candy as bait to lure two children out of the store. The boy sported black lederhosen shorts, while the girl wore a German dirndl. Waiting for them on the sidewalk was the Reluctant Dragon. As Jake and the two kids climbed onto the dragon's back, Jo couldn't help but grin. "Jake has Hansel and Gretel and is using the Reluctant Dragon as an Uber."

Once again, the reporter appeared on-screen, long enough to introduce one more video. "And what was perhaps the most concerning event in downtown today was partially captured on a police officer's body camera." Black and white footage showed someone running after the Tahoe Jo had commandeered as it plowed down the sidewalk. People were screaming and leaping out of the way. The reporter spoke over the video. "Luckily, no pedestrians were injured in this event, but the dangerous lion that police tried to subdue is still on the loose somewhere in Boston."

"I'm certainly not in Kansas anymore," Dorothy said quietly.

Jo turned off her phone and thought about how bizarre this all must seem from Dorothy's perspective. But Jo was also trying to imagine how in the world she was ever going to round up all the characters. Even Silas wouldn't stand a chance at catching Mowgli, the man-cub, with that kind of agility. Her goal to get all the characters safe and in one place seemed nearly impossible.

"Nothing is as it should be," Dorothy said, pointing to Jo's phone. "Tiny people in a tiny thing. And they look nothing like the munchkins I know."

"I can only imagine how strange all of this must be to you," Jo said.

Dorothy nodded. "Yes. Very. Ever since the cyclone picked Toto and me up and carried us away. The spinning and twirling and falling …"

"Scared? Alone? Not sure if you can trust what you're seeing or hearing?" Jo said.

"That's right," Dorothy said.

"I've been feeling that way myself," Jo said. "When your world is spinning out of your control, it's scary."

"I talk to Toto when I'm scared," Dorothy said.

"I talk to my mouse, Nimble," Jo told her.

Dorothy giggled. "You have a mouse?"

Jo nodded and smiled. "He's a little rascal, but he's always been there for me."

"It's good to have a best friend to talk to," Dorothy said.

"Yes, it is." Jo still couldn't believe she was sitting here with Dorothy, having this conversation.

"You've already been such a big help to us, Jo, but can I ask another favor?" Dorothy said.

"Of course, anything," Jo answered.

"Can you help us find the yellow brick road so we can get to the Emerald City?"

"I'll try. But if we can't find the Emerald City, maybe you all can stay here with me."

Dorothy sighed. "I would love to stay with you, Jo, but I really need to get home. I left Aunt Em and Uncle Henry without telling them I love them. I left before I realized I didn't need to leave at all."

Jo studied the girl beside her and tried to commit every detail of the moment to memory. Then she blinked back tears at the goodbye she knew was inevitable. If only things were different and we could really stay best friends forever, she thought.

"I promise I'll do everything I can to make sure you get home to your Aunt Em and Uncle Henry."

Dorothy put her hand on Jo's arm. "Thank you, Jo. You are indeed a good witch."

Jo glanced over at the other Oz characters, all fast asleep. "I could talk to you all night, but I think we should get some rest."

With a weary sigh, Dorothy slipped off her shoes and lay down beside Jo. In a soft whisper, she wished Jo good night. Jo whispered back, "Sweet dreams, Dorothy."

As the moon gracefully slipped behind a passing cloud, a mysterious and ethereal darkness settled upon the tranquil streets of Boston. Illuminated only by sporadic streetlights, a large black moving truck glided stealthily down the hushed suburban road flanked by neatly lined houses. Almost imperceptible, yet eerily captivating, the haunting melody of Swan Lake whispered through the night air, gently seeping into the homes and stirring the sleeping souls within ... until, one by one, the characters ... awoke.

Chapter 16
The Road Less Traveled

"Once upon a midnight dreary, while I pondered, weak and weary, over many a quaint and curious volume of forgotten lore, while I nodded, nearly napping, suddenly there came a tapping, as of someone gently rapping …"

Jo fought her way out of a deep sleep and, in her dreamy brain fog, registered the persistent sound of SQUEAKING and SCRATCHING.

She mumbled with her eyes still closed, "Nimble, it's too early …" The scratching continued.

Reluctantly, she pried her eyes open, only to find a tiny street mouse scratching his claws at the side of Toto's basket. "Where on earth did you come from?" she questioned, but the mouse scurried away in a flash. As Jo sat up, the events of the previous night came rushing back and, with it, panic. She was all alone. Leaping to her feet, she scanned the room.

"Dorothy? Are you in here? Tin Woodman? Scarecrow?" She

heard the worried sound in her own voice. Then, she spotted a pair of gleaming silver shoes on one side of Toto's basket; the oil can was inside, but the dog wasn't. On the other side of the basket was Tin Woodman's axe.

Jo and her cohorts had agreed to meet at her house that morning with all the characters they'd rounded up. Grabbing her phone, she quickly sent a text to the group: Oz characters mysteriously missing.

Her phone pinged with texts as everyone chimed in. New plan. Java the Hut in an hour.

Jo, Polly, Sara, Jake, and Noah were gathered around a small table tucked in the corner of Java the Hut coffee shop.

Noah absently tapped Aladdin's lamp, sitting on the table in front of him, and looked at his friends. "When I started getting texts from you guys saying that your characters were gone, I was relieved. I thought I was going nuts and had imagined the whole thing!" He tightened the knot of Aladdin's silk sash, which was tied around his head. "I mean, who goes rug shopping only to find themselves suddenly airborne? One moment we're in the store, and the next, we're soaring through the sky on a magic carpet. What a rush! Couldn't even tell you how high we flew, but it was the coolest experience I've ever had."

Polly nodded, her large black bow bouncing with each

movement. "I loved spending time with Snow White. Being part of that magical adventure felt incredible. Though I must admit, those little men in my basement, with their constant clanging and banging, made it impossible to get a good night's sleep." She pointed to the two tools sitting beside her. "They left these behind."

"I'm kind of thad," Sara said. "My guyth didn't leave a thouvenir for me."

Polly held out the shovel. "Here, Sara. You can have this. I don't need both."

Sara reached for the shovel. "Thankth, Polly."

Jake dug into his pockets, retrieving two handfuls of crumpled candy wrappers. "This is all I've got," he declared incredulously. "It's hard to believe anyone could eat more candy than me, but Hansel and Gretel did it," he exclaimed. "After I helped them onto the back of the Reluctant Dragon—who was super friendly, by the way—I started to climb on behind them. But lost my footing, and before I knew it, they took off without me."

Jo experienced that same whiplash of emotions after waking to find Dorothy was gone. The vibrant colors of the rainbow faded to a dull black and white when her childhood hero vanished. She looked at her friends. "Being with Dorothy... it was more than amazing, you know? I felt this strong connection between us, like we were kindred spirits. I truly believed that she felt the same way ... but then, when I woke up, she was gone … All of them were. Now, Toto doesn't have his basket, and Tin Man is without his oil can and axe." She shifted her gaze down to the shimmering silver shoes on her feet. "And poor Dorothy is without her shoes that have such incredible power."

Sara furrowed her brow. "I just don't get it. How did they all just dithapeare in the middle of the night? And why?"

The group exchanged puzzled glances, each offering their own theories and speculations. Just then, the bell above the coffee shop door jingled, drawing their attention to Drew as he entered. He looked like he'd had a worse night than they had; his hair sprouted bits of grass, and his clothes were wrinkled and covered in dirt.

Drew started toward the counter to order but spotted the book club kids in the back. He made his way to their table.

"Good day, young peasants," he commented. "Your dedication to your passions 'tis admirable."

Jake frowned at him. "Huh?"

"A meeting of the book club on a weekend?" Drew asked.

Despite Drew looking disheveled and dirty, Jo couldn't stop the flush creeping up her face. She looked away from Drew, wishing he wouldn't notice her embarrassment.

"Nothing personal, but you look kind of … terrible," Noah said.

Drew sighed and rubbed his temples. "I'm afraid I feel the way I appear. Terrible. My head is throbbing with pain, so I've come into this fine establishment to get a strong cup of roasted beans and hope that will help what ails me," he admitted.

"You're talking pretty weird, dude," Jake said. "You suddenly gone British?"

Drew looked sheepish. "Sorry. I'm a thespian at heart, and when I'm in character, it's hard to break the habit. Maybe I'd be a little sharper if I hadn't slept in the forest last night."

Jo's brows shot up. "You slept in the forest?"

Drew nodded, a mischievous grin spreading across his face. "Yep."

"Why?" Jo asked.

"I met this incredible guy yesterday, a brilliant actor. He was so convincing that I genuinely felt like I was hanging out with R.H. himself. He never broke character. We formed our own band of men with some bikers and made the world a better place by robbing the rich and giving to the homeless. It was like being in a twelve-hour stage production. I'm convinced now I'd rather be in a Broadway show than act in a film. It was seriously the best day of my life! Well, except for this raging headache of mine," he added with a slight grimace. "See you guys later."

Band of men? R.H.? Jo frowned. Is it possible ...?

As Drew turned to leave and grab some much-needed coffee from the nearby counter, Jo caught sight of something peculiar across his back.

"Drew! Wait!" she exclaimed. "That bow … did you get it from R.H., as in Robin Hood?"

Drew pulled the bow from his shoulder. "Cool, right? I think it was his way of thanking me for hanging with him all day in Sherwood Forest. That's what he called Franklin Park."

"I'm sure he appreciated spending the day with you, but there's no way Robin Hood would have left his bow and quiver behind," Jo said. "In fact, now that I'm really thinking about it, there's no way Dorothy would have left her shoes or Toto's basket. None of the characters would have left their things behind. It just doesn't make sense."

Drew frowned. "I'm confused. Did you guys spend the day with actors, too?"

Polly started humming a tune. At first, it was a soft melody, but her humming gradually grew louder. Jo spoke over her.

"Robin Hood wasn't an actor. He's a person as real as you and me …" Jo said. "Remember when I told you I needed to save the characters yesterday?"

"Sure," Drew said. "No offense, but you sounded a little crazy."

Jo sighed. "So I've been told."

"Though the World Health Organization has determined one in four will experience a mental health disorder, she's not one of them," Jake said.

"O-kay," Drew said. "Whatever."

"You don't have to believe me," Jo said, shooting an irritated look at Polly, who was humming even louder. "Polly? I appreciate your perpetual optimism, but right now isn't the best time to be humming name that tune!"

"Sorry. I guess I was just trying to lighten the mood. There is nothing in the world so irresistibly contagious as laughter and good humor … and a good hum."

Jo sighed and nodded. "You're right, sorry, I …"

But before Jo could finish her thought, Sara interjected, attempting to identify the familiar tune. "Polly … ith that 'Twan Lake' you were humming?"

Polly shrugged. "I don't know. But it's like the background music to everything in my head."

Noah suddenly chimed in, his eyes widening with realization. "Mine too! I heard that melody in my dreams last night."

Jake nodded. "Me too," he confessed. "It's like the music has been haunting me."

"Now that you guys mention it," Jo said, "I've been hearing it too."

Drew, his curiosity now piqued by the discussion, looked equally astonished. "Umm. That's weird," he commented, his voice tinged with uncertainty. "I heard it, too."

At Drew's comment, Jo fell silent, lost in thought. *Swan Lake! The music is a necessary part of my creative process.*

Polly tapped her on the arm. "Penny for your thoughts, Jo."

She turned to Polly and exclaimed, "I think you've solved the mystery!"

"I have?" Polly said. "Well, then, good for me!" She grinned. "Wait. What mystery did I solve?"

"Why our characters left in the middle of the night, leaving behind their most valuable things," Jo explained.

Drew sat down in the nearest chair. "I am so confused. Explain, please."

"In the journal I found in my basement, the author mentioned a melody that he always played while he was crafting his characters. He believed it brought him a sense of tranquility and enhanced his creativity. That melody was Swan Lake."

Drew rubbed his temples. "I feel like I just flew over the cuckoo's nest."

The other kids exchanged glances.

"The characters followed the music," Noah said.

Jo nodded. "And whatever Silas has planned for them won't be good. We need to save them."

"So, the book club to the rescue?" Drew asked.

"That's the plan," Jo said. "You can join the club and help us."

"You got a name for your club?"

"We never picked one," Sara said.

"How about 'White Rose Book Club,'" Jo suggested.

Jake shook his head. "Pansy name."

"White Rose was the name of the group of students who put their lives on the line to defy Hitler in World War Two," Jo said.

"It's got my vote," Noah said. The others nodded.

Drew looked at Jo. "I'm in. What now?"

"Now we head to the Big Top Domain."

Chapter 17
Tasty, Tasty Beautiful Fear

The colossal expanse of the Big Top Domain was truly striking. It featured sleek, futuristic body scanners that stood like imposing metal sentinels on either side of the tent entrance. Several smaller tents flanked a pathway leading to the main attraction, a towering canvas dome crowned with a massive flag. Emblazoned upon the flag were two striking white initials—SS, resembling electrified lightning bolts.

Jo and her friends nestled in the cover of the trees, their eyes fixed on the entrance. A long line of eager teens stood waiting, each clutching a book—their ticket for admission—impatient to enter what had been advertised as an astonishing techno experience. Even from their stealthy position, they felt the excitement rippling through the crowd. The air was festive, almost party-like, and the upbeat music reminded Jo of the last time she'd been roller skating. The aromas of popcorn and cotton candy floated past on a breeze and lent to the feeling that whatever was inside would be worth the wait.

"Pretty large turnout," Jo said.

"I love the circus," Polly said. "But I've never used a book as a ticket."

"We won't get inside here without one," Sara said.

"We have a bigger problem," Jo observed. "There are metal detectors at the entrance."

"That's no big deal," Jake said. "It's like at the airport. They use Advanced Imaging Technology. You know, a millimeter wave scanner that detects a wide range of metallic and nonmetallic threats in seconds. It's completely harmless."

"Harmless?" Jo said. "Not if you're carrying weapons."

The realization hit Jake, and he quickly glanced at the group's collection. "Umm. Yeah. Pretty sure a shovel and a bow aren't on the approved list to bring inside."

"We can't go through the scanner with this stuff," Drew said. "That's for sure."

"We could ditch it," Noah said.

"No! We can't do that. These things don't belong to us. Their rightful owners need them back," Jo argued. "Not to mention they might come in handy."

"There has to be a solution," Polly said. "There's an answer to every problem."

"We just have to find a different way in," Jo said. "I wish we knew more about the layout of the place."

"There's a sequence of tents you must go through," Jake said. "The first one is over there." He pointed to one of the smaller tents to the left.

"How did you know that?" Noah asked.

Jake frowned and hesitated while he rubbed absently at the back of his neck. "Someone posted it."

"I didn't see it," Noah said.

"Guess you just missed it," Jake said, avoiding eye contact with his friends. "Anyway, some of the posts about this place are insider tips."

"You see any insider tips about how to sneak into one of those tents?" Jo asked.

Jake shrugged. "No, sorry. We'll just have to figure that out on our own."

A copper arrowhead pierced through the tent's fabric, leaving a three-inch hole. Moments later, a curious eyeball appeared in the opening and peeked into the surroundings. It quickly surveyed the area, glancing to the right and then to the left. As it conducted its reconnaissance, impatient whispers echoed nearby.

"Can you see anything?" one voice asked eagerly.

"Sort of," the eyeball responded.

"What do you see?" inquired a third voice.

Outside the tent, Jo leaned away from the hole and blinked before pressing her eye against the canvas again. "I think they're watching a movie."

"What kind of movie? Anything we know?" Noah asked.

Jo shook her head but kept her eye pressed against the canvas. "I don't think so. It's too distorted to tell. Like it's out of focus or something."

Jake, looking a bit sheepish, offered another insight. "Could be like those 3-D movies. You've got to have those special glasses to see what's really going on."

Jo leaned away from the tent. "Yeah, but how do we get our hands on those goggles?"

"I've got mine," Jake blurted out.

The group turned to him with looks of confusion.

Jake sighed. "I came here last night after I got all amped up on candy. I just wanted to see what it's all about." He reached into his back pocket and pulled out a pair of goggles.

"Confession is good for the soul," Polly said.

"Why didn't you juth thay tho?" Sara asked.

Jake shrugged. "I dunno. Felt like you guys would judge me or something."

"Me firth." Sara snatched the goggles from him and slid them into place. She looked around and frowned. "I don't thee anything different."

Jake pointed at the hole in the canvas. "Look through there."

Sara peeked through the tear in the tent. "Whoa! Thith ith amathing! Ith not dithtorted at all!"

"What are you seeing, Sara?" Polly asked impatiently.

"Beauty! Tho much beauty!" Sara stepped back and offered the glasses to Polly. "You have to thee it for yourthelf."

Polly put on the goggles and looked through the hole in the tent. "Oh my gosh. It's like nothing I've ever seen. It's like the whole tent is part of the movie! The sky looks like it never ends. And everyone looks so happy. So joyful." Polly laughed. "There's a gorgeous rainbow, and kids are flying kites. The fields are full of sunflowers and poppies. And the colors. So vibrant!"

"Let me see," Noah demanded.

Reluctantly, Polly stepped back and handed him the goggles. Noah took off his own glasses and slipped them on. His reaction was almost identical to the girls'. "Wow! The grass in that field is such a dazzling green it's almost glowing. I'd love to play a game of Quidditch against that beautiful sky!"

Jake grinned. "It makes you want to live there."

Drew poked Noah on the shoulder. "Hey. Can I have a turn?"

With his face pressed against the canvas, Drew let out a low whistle. "I wouldn't mind living in that world!"

He stepped back and offered the glasses to Jo. "You've got to see this, Jo." But she shook her head. "I'm not buying it. Not if Silas is involved. It's got to be some kind of trick. We need to focus and remember why we're here."

"Maybe we have Silas all wrong," Polly said. "He might really just want kids to have a good time at his techno circus."

"No way," Jo said. "He's got the characters, and he told me he'd destroy them. We have to save them."

"Have you got a plan?" Drew asked.

"I say we go straight to the Big Top and find them," Jo said.

But Jake was already shaking his head. "It doesn't work that way. Each of the tents leading to the Big Top is a level of the ultimate end game." He pointed at the tent. "You have to make it through this one to get to the next level. Security won't let us skip a level."

"What's the next level?" Jo asked.

"Suiting up." Jake looked apologetic. "But that's as far as I got last night before I … chickened out."

"So we shimmy under the canvas and then go suit up," Jo said. "And then make our way to the Big Top."

"There's another problem," Drew said. "We only have one pair of goggles."

"We're screwed," Noah exclaimed.

"Maybe not," Jake said. "Last night when the movie ended, there was a moment when the tent went pitch black. I couldn't see a thing. Since we know it's going to happen ..."

"Are you suggesting we steal someone else's goggles?" Polly sounded offended.

"It's the only way we can get them without going through the metal detectors," Jake said. "So, yes, that's exactly what I'm suggesting."

Chapter 18
Truth Is Stranger Than Fiction

One by one, Jo and her friends slipped under the tent's canvas, where a couple hundred teens wearing goggles sat spellbound by the enchanting images on the big screen.

Staying low in an army-type crawl, the gang moved behind the teens seated in the last row. Jake, wearing his goggles, peeked around the corner of the row to gauge when the film would end. Watching intently, he raised four fingers to signal the others and began a countdown, lowering them one by one.

Without warning, the room plunged into darkness, startling the audience—all except Jo and her cohorts. Amid the whispers and speculations, several teens yelled in protest as they felt their goggles being ripped from their heads.

As the lights flickered back on, five furious teens wondered aloud about their missing goggles while the members of the White Rose book club quickly followed Jake toward the exit leading to the next tent.

Jo surveyed the area, where dozens of steel gray lockers lined the circular canvas of the tent. She tried one of the doors.

"Locked."

Polly frowned. "This tent isn't very pretty."

"Pretty boring," Sara chimed in.

"What now, Jake?" Noah asked.

"Wait for it." Jake pointed to an intercom speaker suspended near the apex of the tent. Almost immediately, a disembodied female voice filled the space.

"Welcome. The lockers are now available for you to open."

They heard the locks disengage, and the kids all stepped up to a locker and opened the door. Inside was a black, full-body harness with adjustable straps.

"Wow. Very cool," Drew said.

"Your body harness is equipped with haptic feedback," the voice explained. "Numerous actuators simulate touch, pressure, and movement, allowing you to feel sensations like impacts, textures, and even temperature changes as you interact with the virtual world."

"I don't know about thith," Sara said nervously.

"Shh," Jo said. "They might be listening to us."

Sara nodded, and the female voice on the intercom continued.

"There are also integrated sensors such as accelerometers, gyroscopes, and magnetometers that track your movements in real-time, translating physical actions into the virtual space."

"So awesome!" Noah said.

"In addition," the voice said, "there are biometric sensors monitoring your physiological responses such as heart rate, respiration, and muscle activity. Once suited up, please step forward into the next chamber."

The voice on the intercom went silent, and the kids looked at each other. Polly pulled her harness from the locker. "So many straps and buckles."

"It could uth thome color. Black ithn't my favorite," Sara said.

Drew was already stepping into his harness. "Think I can leave the bow and quiver here in a locker for safekeeping?"

"Good idea. We could put the other things in there as well," Jo said.

Drew collected everything and placed them inside the locker. "What do you suppose is next?"

"I don't know," Jake said nervously. "Like I told you, this is where I bailed."

They emerged from the locker tent through a door into an octagonal room surrounded by solid walls on all sides. It was standing room only, with teens packed like sardines. A large door behind Jo closed swiftly with a whoosh, followed by a thud as the door locked in place. The teens in the tent whispered together in anticipation of what might happen next.

Then, another disembodied voice rang out from a speaker on the ceiling. "Your mission is to defeat the enemy and cross over into the promised land in ten, nine, eight, seven …" As the countdown continued, Polly leaned closer to Jo.

"Promised land?" she whispered.

"We'll be okay," Jo said with more confidence than she felt.

The voice from above continued. "Four, three, two … one! Become your best! Step up to the Test!"

A massive door on the opposite side of the room slid open, propelling the teens into a vibrant cyberpunk world filled with neon-lit alleys, an inky black sky, and towering holographic images. The electronic music pulsated with a deafening volume, causing the ground beneath their feet to vibrate.

As Jo and her friends took in the scene before them, they watched what appeared to be an army of otherworldly AI entities ordering teens around like slaves.

"I want to go back," Sara said.

"You can't go back," Jake told her. "We have to go forward."

"Umm, guys? Our suits look different now," Polly said.

Jo quickly realized her plain clothes and body harness had morphed into a uniform with metallic hues in gunmetal gray. Lightweight body armor covered the chest area. On her sleeves were the SS lightning bolts. When she looked at her friends, she saw they all looked identical, their outfits complete with futurist visors and black boots that had replaced their shoes. In fact, as she took another look at the teens in the room, everyone had taken on the same uniform appearance.

Jake tapped his chest. "Kevlar?"

"What's Kevlar?" Polly asked.

"It's heat resistant; military and law enforcement wear Kevlar vests to protect them from bullets," Jake said.

"Thath thilly," Sara said. "Why would we need protection from—"

"Duck!" Jo yelled as super-heated plasma blasts came flying at them. Jo turned to see the strange AI beings running toward them, firing indiscriminately into the crowd of teens.

The book club group dropped to the ground amid the surrounding chaos. As some of the teen warriors were stuck, their screams echoed in the air. Teens called out to one another, crawling toward each other and tumbling on top of one another as the assault from the AI beings raged on.

How are we supposed to defend ourselves? How can we defeat the enemy and make it to the promised land?

Drew yelled out to Jo as he crawled toward her. "Stay down. Keep low!"

"There's no place to hide," Jo said. "This is insane!"

Drew was close enough now to reach for her hand. Despite all the ruckus, she couldn't ignore the flutter of butterflies in her stomach as their fingers touched.

"This is like shooting fish in a barrel," Drew said. "Stay close, and we'll find a way to sneak around and hit them from behind …"

Before they could react, Jo sensed a sudden change in the goggles. It felt as if a current had surged around the lenses, making her dizzy. At the same moment, Drew let go of her hand. And the butterflies that had been fluttering in her stomach vanished, leaving her overwhelmed with panic.

"Oh no! Not now! Please, Drew … help me!" Through the visor, Drew's eyes had turned yellow; he was no longer himself. Along with the other teens, he was suddenly armed with all sorts of futuristic weapons. Jo couldn't take it any longer. She ripped off the goggles and dropped them to the floor.

Everything in the large tent suddenly appeared different. Jo turned to her friends and, to her horror, they stared back at her with glowing yellow eyes behind the lenses of their goggles.

"You guys! Take them off! Take the goggles off!"

But her frantic pleas fell on deaf ears. The entire room of teens had transformed and were already demonstrating new skills that almost seemed superhuman. They charged at the AI without hesitation, body-slamming them, tossing them aside like puppets—the teens were unstoppable. Jo watched in disbelief as one boy leaped nearly eight feet into the air to jump over a line of AI beings and land on the other side. She couldn't believe what she was witnessing, even as she realized that without the goggles, the cyberpunk world had become a distorted blur of images surrounding the teens, who continued to advance.

Jo was unsure of what to do or where to go. Then she spotted two men in black suits, their pale white complexions accented by dark sunglasses, rushing toward her.

Chapter 19
The Clocks Were Striking Thirteen

Inside the confines of the black semi-trailer, split-screen monitors lined the wall, displaying a combination of the virtual world and reality. Silas reclined comfortably in a burgundy leather chair. Ezra stood dutifully on one side of the chair, and a large German Shepherd rested against him. Absently stroking the dog's head, Silas—wearing a pair of Hugo Boss sunglasses—was fixated on one particular monitor. Jo held his attention as she shimmied under the canvas tent and sprinted to conceal herself behind one of several enormous metal storage containers.

Silas spoke with sinister determination, his words dripping with malice. "Bring her to me, now."

Ezra promptly left the trailer, leaving Silas alone. Leaning forward in his chair, his gaze glued to the monitor, watching as Jo emerged from her hiding spot and rounded a corner at a swift pace. He had an air of certainty about him. "Those silver shoes won't save you, my dear." Silas grinned. "You can run, but you can't hide."

Jo maneuvered between the tightly packed tents, her heart pounding. She finally stopped to catch her breath. Cautiously, she peered out from behind the shadowy black canvas. To her relief, there was no sign of the men that had been chasing her.

Overwhelmed by the weight of her mission, Jo leaned against the tent, her eyes brimming with frustrated tears.

"It's all gone wrong," she whispered. "My friends... the characters."

Out of nowhere, a flash of blue-and-white gingham caught Jo's attention. Her heart skipped a beat as she muttered under her breath, "Dorothy?" Fueled by the hope of reuniting with her lost companion, Jo stayed close to the protective cover of the tents; her gaze fixated on the path that Dorothy had taken. Suddenly, the familiar figure disappeared between the two tents.

In a hushed yet urgent voice, Jo called out, "Dorothy! Wait!"

Jo's heart raced as she desperately tried to keep up with Dorothy. Her companion made another turn, and without a second thought, Jo burst into a run. She darted down a row of black semi-trailers parked behind the midway.

As Jo rounded the corner, there was another flash of Dorothy's dress at the top of a set of stairs leading into a black trailer. She froze, contemplating what might lie inside. Yet, she was determined in her mission to rescue Dorothy and summoned the courage to climb the steps. Taking a deep breath, she stepped through the open door, her heart pounding.

Jo entered the trailer. A row of monitors lined one wall facing a burgundy captain's chair next to a desk. Jo walked toward the desk, where an old Underwood manual typewriter sat next to a box filled with neatly typed paper. The top page read: A Manifesto by Silas Schutzstaffel. Curious, Jo turned to the first page. The same three words were repeated over and over, filling the entire page: Discipline. Order. Power. As she flipped through the pages, she saw nothing but those three words.

Behind her, the door clicked shut. Spinning around, she faced Ezra, a smile on his face.

"Welcome," he said.

Jo swung her gaze around and spotted Wulf, the German Shepherd, who issued a low growl and stared at her with piercing yellow eyes.

Chapter 20
Terror Made Me Cruel

Jo stifled a scream, scanning the room for another way out. Her eyes landed on Silas, who was across the room, standing in front of a full-length mirror, staring intently at his own reflection. If he was aware of her presence, he didn't show it.

She watched as he raised his arms over his head, lowered them slowly, and shifted his feet into a wider stance. His whole theatrical demeanor gave her the creeps. When Jo finally spoke up, she hoped Silas wouldn't notice the fear in her voice.

"What have you done with Dorothy?" she demanded.

Silas didn't turn from the mirror but raised his right index finger to silence her. He then extended his right arm, palm facing outward. A shiver ran down Jo's spine. Silas kept his gaze on his reflection for a moment longer before turning to face her. His eyes were glowing yellow.

"Ah, Miss March, so good of you to join me," he said.

Jo swallowed hard. "Your eyes … they're …"

"A direct result from the Powder of Life," he said. "But let's keep that our little secret, shall we?"

"I don't understand," Jo stammered. "You were ... are ... wax?"

"No. Flesh and bone, just like you. Well, almost just like you."

"I still don't understand."

"And I don't care," Silas replied. "Let's talk about my Big Top Domain. What do you think of it?"

"Evil," Jo said.

Silas chuckled. "Well put. But you haven't truly experienced it as it was intended."

Jo looked around the room, searching for any sign of her friend. "I don't want to experience it. I just want Dorothy. Where is she?"

Silas looked amused. "Your eyes must have been playing tricks on you, my dear." As Jo watched, Silas gracefully moved past the wall of high-tech monitors displaying a flurry of images.

Jo begged. "Please. I just want my friends and the characters back!"

Silas moved toward her. "That's a very big ask, don't you think?"

Jo took a step back. "No. I'm asking you to do the right thing."

"It's not right for me," Silas said. "The right thing for me is the Powder of Life. Give it to me, and you can have what you want."

"I want Dorothy and the rest of the characters," she said. "And all my friends."

"Yes, yes, so you've said." Silas sighed. "I'm losing my patience with you, Miss March. You have no choice but to hand me the powder. Here. Now."

"I don't have it with me," Jo said.

"I believe you're a very smart young lady," Silas said. "And I also believe you're lying to me. I know you have the Powder of Life with you."

"Why would I risk bringing it?"

"Why risk not bringing it? You might need it. You want the characters back, don't you?"

Jo's expression gave her away. Silas laughed. "You're smart, but your emotions are very transparent. Now, give me the powder."

Jo shook her head stubbornly. "Not without my friends and the characters—all unharmed."

Silas glared at her, his yellow eyes glowing even brighter with his anger. Fear crept up her spine. He studied her for a few moments, and then, finally, he sighed.

"You are the most determined young lady I've ever met," he admitted begrudgingly. "So, I concede." He offered a dubious smile and bowed slightly in Jo's direction. "You win." Silas turned to Ezra and gave him an insider's nod.

Ezra opened the door, and, to Jo's amazement, Dorothy stepped into the room with a black velvet bag over her head.

Jo called out to her. "Dorothy! It's me, Jo. Are you alright?"

Dorothy nodded but didn't say a word. Silas held out his hand. "We made a deal. Give me the powder."

"What are you going to use it for?"

"For me to know and you to find out."

"How can I trust you'll let me leave with Dorothy?" Jo asked.

"I give you my word. You will be allowed to leave with that character." Silas snapped his fingers. "The powder."

With trembling hands, Jo lifted the lanyard over her head to reveal the pouch holding the powder. Silas issued a deep, satisfied sigh. "Ezra."

Ezra grabbed the pouch from Jo. "Got it, boss."

"I'd like to go now."

Silas waved her away. "Go. Leave."

"First, I need to know where to find the rest of the characters and my friends. You gave me your word," Jo said.

"I said you could leave with that character." Silas smiled, and it unnerved her. She hurried toward the character. "It'll be okay, Dorothy," she reassured, gently removing the black velvet bag. Her knees nearly buckled as she stared at an imposing man whose face was as pale as the pages of a book. He, too, had yellow eyes, just like Silas.

She spun to accuse Silas. "You lied!"

"I never said it was your precious Dorothy. Allow me to introduce one of my Wordmen. Show her."

The Wordman ripped off the dress, exposing his bare chest adorned with words inked in black: Discipline, Order, Power, repeated over and over again.

"You're an evil, despicable, lying coward."

"I take offense at the word coward." Silas cocked his head to the side. "I must admit, Miss March, you have spunk. Perhaps even more spunk than the Josephine March in Little Women."

Surprised, Jo looked at Silas in disbelief. He raised an eyebrow, confirming her shock. "That's right, I've read it. And then I burned it, along with hundreds of other books."

Confused, Jo asked, "Why?"

"Because I hate them and everything they represent. Because they paint innocence as if it's a virtue, and, most importantly because they are an impediment to the SS Youth Movement."

Jo couldn't help but ask, "Youth movement?"

He gestured to a table in the room. "Allow me to show you my plans."

The table held an enormous military field map that stretched across its entire surface. A tall push pin was stuck into the city of Boston, proudly displaying an SS flag.

"The crusade begins here, Miss March, but it will not end in Boston. Its reach will extend to every corner of the country."

Sickened, Jo finally understood the twisted gravity of his evil plan. "You're ... recruiting," she whispered, horrified.

Silas picked up a small container from the table. "Very astute of you, Miss March. And once my recruits across the country are in place, a simple phone call will trigger the hypnotic phrase they will be programmed to receive to make them instruments of my bidding. You see, 'The world breaks everyone, and afterward, many are strong at the broken places.'"

He took a pair of contacts from the container and slipped them in. His eyes went from yellow to black. Turning to Jo, he asked, "A good look for me, don't you agree?"

Repulsed, Jo said, "You're insane!"

"Insanity suggests a lack of clarity, a lack of knowing what one desires. That could not be further from the truth in my case."

Jo's voice trembled with fear as she resorted to desperate reasoning. "You should never have experienced the Powder of Life."

A dark smile played on Silas' lips. "You'll need to take that up with my creator. Oh, wait... you can't. I exterminated him. And soon, my name will be on the lips of every person across this once beautiful country and eventually around the world."

Jo shook her head. "It'll never work. 'There is some good in the world, and it's worth fighting for.'"

Silas laughed. "Oh, my dear Jo, you can quote Mr. Tolkien all you want, but it's already working," he replied arrogantly. "Future SS Warriors are being trained as we speak." He glanced at his watch, a glint of excitement in his eyes. "I've enjoyed our little tête-à-tête, Miss March, but now the leader has an army to address. Ezra!" Silas growled. "Take Miss March back to the lockers and see to it that she returns her harness."

"Yes, Boss," Ezra said.

Ezra tried to take Jo by the arm, but she yanked it away.

Jo looked at Silas defiantly. "I'm not leaving without my friends or the characters."

Silas glared at her. "You are under the misguided notion that you have a choice in the matter, and I'm here to tell you that you do not."

Silas motioned for Ezra to go. "After she returns my property, make sure she leaves the premises!"

This time, Ezra grabbed Jo's harness and tugged on it. "Let's go."

Deeply disappointed in her failed mission, Jo's eyes swam with tears. She was letting everyone down. *Dorothy! I'm so sorry ...*

Chapter 21
Open Your Eyes

As they approached the tent with the lockers, Ezra signaled to two Wordmen who were standing guard. He gave Jo a little push toward them.

"Take her inside and make sure she leaves the harness, then escort her off the property. Don't let her out of your sight. She's a sneaky one!" Ezra instructed.

The Wordmen nodded in unison. Ezra sneered at Jo. "Pretty bold of you to think you could outsmart the boss, little girl. You got guts, though, that's for sure."

As Ezra slinked away, the Wordmen motioned for Jo to enter the tent.

Once inside, one of the Wordmen yanked impatiently on her harness. Jo pulled away from him.

"Okay, okay," she said. "I'm doing it."

Taking her time to unbuckle the harness, she struggled to

remember which locker Drew had stashed the weapons in. As she scanned them, it hit her that Drew's locker was just one space away from hers. She approached what she hoped was the right locker and opened it a crack. Jackpot! All the characters' treasures were still inside. She knew they wouldn't let her leave with the weapons. Weapons! Two axes, a lamp, a bow, and a shovel.

Jo addressed the Wordmen. "Would you mind turning around? I need to change back into my other clothes."

The Wordmen exchanged glances, weighing her request. The taller one shrugged, and they did as she asked, turning their backs to her. Jo didn't hesitate. She grabbed the shovel. I don't want to kill 'em, but I do need them to take a nap!

Swinging the shovel as hard as she could, she knocked out the first Wordman and took out the second before he knew what hit him.

"Sleep tight, you weirdos," she said.

Grabbing everything from the locker, she opened the tent door a crack and peered out. Dashing out of the tent, she was already formulating a plan.

As all eyes were glued on the main event in the Big Top, no one noticed when the back of the black canvas lifted a few inches off the ground, allowing several items to be pushed inside the tent. First came a shovel, followed by a pickaxe, a bow, a silver axe, and a lamp. Once the pile was complete, Jo shimmied under the canvas and took a second to get her bearings. She had entered behind the bleachers that stretched all the way to the peak of the tent.

Jo couldn't go around to the front where she might be seen, nor could she remain on the ground without a clear vantage point.

What would dad tell me? Nothing ventured, nothing gained, munchkin. She knew he wouldn't approve of the plan that had just hatched in her head. But there was only one option left. She had to climb up.

It had seemed like a solid plan: to scale the back of the bleachers until she reached a place at the top where she could see everything. Secured in her harness, Jo had attached Aladdin's lamp to one of the clips, tucked Tin Woodman's silver axe in her pocket, slung the bow over her shoulder, and threaded the shovel's handle through the back armholes of her vest, so it rested horizontally. She used the pickaxe to hook onto the metal bracing of each row of bleachers as she climbed higher. But halfway up, doubt crept in—she feared she wouldn't make it. The weapons felt heavy and cumbersome. Looking down only fueled her anxiety. Bad idea, Jo! Stupid idea! Don't look down. Look up!

With sheer determination, she willed herself to push on until she finally reached the top, where, to her relief, no one was seated. Climbing over the top row, she dropped into one of the seats, grateful for the shadows that cloaked her presence beneath the tent's peak.

Her gaze swept across the magnificent scene before her. The tent, filled with electric energy, soared to impressive heights, reaching over a hundred feet at its center. There was intricate rigging hanging from a sturdy steel bale ring that encircled the towering center poles.

Her attention was soon drawn to a large wooden stage in the center. Its nondescript appearance contrasted with the captivating sight of a glass tank positioned upon it. Measuring eight by three feet, the tank was nearly filled to the top with inky-black water, creating a strange and mysterious presence.

Suddenly, there he was. Silas, the master of ceremonies, made his grand entrance. Impeccably dressed in his gray doubled-breasted jacket and black trousers, he took center stage. As his intense gaze swept over the crowd, the air crackled with anticipation. Time seemed to stand still for a moment, and then Silas raised his arms towards the ceiling, his voice echoing throughout the tent. "Welcome to my Big Top!" The audience sprang to their feet, bursting into enthusiastic applause.

Jo scanned the crowd, her eyes searching for familiar faces. Finally, she spotted Drew in the next section of bleachers; he was on his feet, attention fixed on the stage as Silas captivated the audience.

"Do you feel strong?" Silas boomed.

The crowd screamed back, "I do!"

With her head on a swivel, Jo kept searching for her friends.

She soon noticed Polly and Sara standing a few feet apart, goggles in place, attention fixed on Silas.

Silas continued to pump up the crowd, his energy contagious. "Do you feel powerful?!"

Again, the crowd responded loudly, "I do!"

Silas gazed across the sea of faces, then moved to the end of the stage with a mischievous grin.

"But do you want to feel even more?" he teased, his voice filled with intrigue.

The audience responded instantly, their applause rising like a drumbeat of the show. Jo continued her search for Noah and Jake in the sea of faces until she spotted Noah clapping, his goggles firmly in place.

Turning her gaze back to the stage, Jo's eyes widened as Silas spoke again; his voice was magnetic, commanding attention with its blend of passion and authority. "You're beginning to realize you have this creative potential to reshape this world according to your own vision. But there is a barrier to that transformation: those who have made a mess of our reality. They squander the Divine's resources, poisoning our waters and air. They start wars, weaving webs of lies and deceit. They infiltrate your thoughts with negativity and subject you to the mind-numbing clamor of social media, invading your privacy while demanding unattainable perfection. They overlook the immense pressure you live under, contributing to a world increasingly chaotic and perilous. They are the ultimate hypocrites, and their time has come to an end. This world is in desperate need of a new beginning—one that can only arise through you." He paused, letting his words resonate. "If you can embrace change, if you'll allow me to guide you, we can forge a brighter future together. A harmonious place filled with meaning in this seemingly meaningless existence."

The crowd burst into frenetic applause. Jo looked around as Silas had them eating out of the palms of his hands. Silas dropped his voice to a conspiratorial whisper and leaned toward them. "I'm here to reveal the truth to you," he declared with conviction. "It's time for you to be reborn, just as I have."

On a large screen, the faces of three teenagers appeared. "Now, I'm going to share videos recorded last night by three courageous warriors equipped with their goggles. First up is Cleet Ambrose. Cleet, please stand." As he rose, curious eyes shifted around the tent. "Everyone, direct your attention to the screen."

The kids in the audience watched the screen, where a modestly furnished family room appeared, with a television that looked as though it came from the last century. A reporter on the TV spoke in that serious tone reserved for serious situations. "As you can see, these seemingly innocent-looking children made off with around sixty pounds of candy. And as unbelievable as that may sound, their getaway vehicle was a flying dragon."

Though he wasn't visible, the audience clearly heard Cleet's voice as he mocked the reporter's words. "Innocent-looking children. Sixty pounds of candy. Ha!"

Suddenly, a piercing scream echoed from somewhere within the house. The camera panned off the television to Gladys, a woman in her late seventies, as she rushed into the family room, clutching a wet plate and a dishrag.

Panic-stricken, she cried out, "Cleet!"

"What?" said the disembodied voice.

In a state of hysteria, Gladys yelled, "There's a wolf in our backyard! And it's wearing a nightie!"

"Probably just your reflection in the window, Gran." Cleet chuckled.

Quiet, almost nervous laughter rippled through the audience.

Quick as a flash, Gladys stormed across the room with angry, determined strides. She swiftly grabbed hold of Cleet's ear and twisted it hard, causing him to yelp in pain. Without missing a beat, she forcefully dragged him towards the window, pressing his face against the glass.

There, beneath the tree in the backyard, was the wolf, comfortably nestled in a flannel nightgown, licking its chops.

Gladys, her voice filled with a mix of panic and grief,

exclaimed, "That reflection just ate our cat! Poor Mrs. Whiskers!"

The video remained fixed on the wolf for a moment longer and then moved to Cleet's grandmother, her eyes squinted in anger. Pointing a bony finger at him, she warned sternly, "With that attitude, I'm telling you right now, you aren't going back to that stupid Big Top carnival, no sirree ... stupid boy. Now get rid of that wolf before he tries to eat Mr. Huckleberry!"

Gladys turned and walked away, shaking her head. "What is wrong with this world? Wolves aren't supposed to eat cats!"

Gladys walked out of the room, and the camera went back to focus on Cleet at the window, looking at the wolf. With his face reflected in the window, the kids in the audience could clearly see Cleet wearing his goggles. He grinned. "You're right! That wolf is supposed to eat somebody's grandma!"

The video ended, and laughter filled the tent. Silas surveyed his audience with a satisfied gaze. "To truly laugh you must be able to take your pain and play with it!" As he had planned, the tension from the kids had eased with the laughter. The more relaxed, the easier to manipulate.

Silas raised his hands, and the crowd grew quiet. "We can endure anything as long as we make fun of it. Cleet, come forward!"

As Cleet made his way to the stage, Silas addressed his future warriors. "Without commitment, without dedication, nothing will change." When Cleet reached the stage, Silas turned to him. "Are you prepared to take the next step? To venture where very few have dared to go?"

Cleet nodded adamantly. "I am!"

Leaning forward in her seat, Jo watched as Ezra and two Wordmen appeared before Silas, diligently attaching metal cables to Cleet's harness.

The audience fell into an eerie silence. Without warning, Cleet was hoisted high, until he was suspended over the tank filled with the ominously dark water. Suddenly, the harness released from the cables, and Cleet plummeted into the depths of the ink-black liquid. As he vanished beneath the surface, the audience held their breath, waiting to see what would unfold next.

Chapter 22
What Fresh Hell Is This

As each second ticked by, Cleet remained submerged. The teens continued leaning forward in eager anticipation. Jo, consumed with anxiety about Cleet's fate, couldn't take her eyes off the unfolding scene.

Finally, the two Wordmen approached the glass enclosure. One of them unfastened the latch at the front, causing the door to swing open. A torrential flow of inky-black water gushed forth, flooding the stage and cascading onto the floor below.

Cleet lay motionless. Silas approached and turned to Ezra, who took a small spoon, dipped it into the pouch containing the Powder of Life, and handed it to him. Kneeling beside Cleet, Silas removed his goggles and blew the powder into Cleet's face. "Rise," Silas commanded.

Moments later, Cleet gasped for air. When his eyes finally opened, they glowed a brilliant yellow.

Suddenly, the unmistakable strains of Richard Wagner's "Ride of the Valkyries" reverberated throughout the tent. The crowd held their breath in anticipation. Then, a smile graced Cleet's face as he embarked on a meticulously choreographed dance routine. Behind him, a dozen Wordmen appeared; their dark sunglasses, suitcoats, and shirts were gone. Bold, black words were tattooed all over their pale, white skin, and their glowing yellow eyes were an eerie sight as they provided the perfect backup to Cleet's dance.

Jo admitted to herself that the spectacle of Cleet and the backup dancers was truly mesmerizing.

As the last final notes of "Valkyries" echoed in the air, Silas pointed to the ceiling, where a large, clear sphere opened up, releasing a shower of black ash confetti upon the audience.

Intrigued by the strange confetti, Jo stared at the black, ashen pieces on her arm. Frowning, she reached for a piece and inspected it. To her surprise, fragmented words were scattered within the dark particles.

"Books ..." Jo muttered to herself, her eyes widening with understanding. He burned all the books. Silas stepped into the spotlight. "We must erase the past in order to create a better tomorrow." That was when Jo spotted more Wordmen in the background, escorting her beloved characters—bound with rope— onto the stage.

Silas continued, "I brought the characters from the literary classics here. Each one cherished from your childhood. But should they remain cherished? As I mentioned earlier, we must erase the past to create a better tomorrow."

The tent suddenly filled with a low rumble that grew louder. Jo watched in disbelief as the front of the stage floor split open, revealing a five-foot-wide plank in the center. The sides of the stage rolled back, exposing a massive pit of fire. Angry flames of reddish-orange danced in the air. A wave of nausea washed over Jo. She realized Silas planned to destroy the characters, and now she knew how he was going to do it.

Chapter 23
It Was a Pleasure to Burn

Silas signaled for two Wordmen. "Let's begin!"

Two Wordmen began to untie Pinocchio from the rest of the characters.

"STOP!"

Jo's voice sliced through the tension, and Silas saw all eyes turn toward her as she made her way down the bleachers.

Ugh, Silas thought, rolling his eyes. That rotten kid! I thought I got rid of her!

"Hey, everyone! I know we've been told to keep moving forward and forget the past, but we can't ignore where we came from! Our history is like a quilt stitched together, filled with our stories, wins, and losses. Every story shows us who we are and reminds us of our roots. These characters from our favorite books and tales helped shape us, and we must protect them no matter what!"

Silas sensed a shift in the crowd's energy; their faith in him was waning. He had to take swift action before all his plans unraveled. He pulled a tiny remote device with a bright red button from his pocket and locked eyes with Jo. With a wicked grin, he pushed the button. In an instant, all the goggles lit up, and the crowd's eyes glowed an electric yellow.

Silas demanded, "Repeat after me … discipline … order … power …"

In perfect unison, the crowd began chanting. "Discipline, order, power!" Their voices swelled with intensity with each repetition. Then, Silas raised his right arm straight into the air, and the entire crowd emulated his salute.

While Jo moved farther down the bleachers, Silas basked in the glory of his army.

Jo, ducking under the outstretched arms of the teens, stopped in front of Polly. She quickly yanked the goggles from her friend's eyes.

"Help, Polly! I need you!"

Polly stared straight ahead in a hypnotic trance and repeated, "Discipline, order, power!"

Jo waved a hand in front of her friend's face. "Polly? It's me, Jo," she said, her voice rising in desperation.

Still nothing, just that blank stare. Jo shook her by the shoulders, but it was like shaking a statue. In a last-ditch effort to break through, she slapped Polly across her cheek. "Wake up!"

Polly blinked and rubbed her cheek, momentarily bewildered, but then a look of recognition illuminated her face. "Jo? Oh my gosh, it's so good to see you!"

Jo pointed toward the stage, her voice urgent. "Silas is going to burn them all! Every last character! We have to save them!" She handed Polly the weapons. "Find the rest of the White Rose Book Club and give them their weapons. Hurry!"

Silas's eyes were on her, tracking her every move as she made her way closer to the stage. Just then, he called out to his captive warriors in a haughty demeanor.

"You see, my warriors, a game is just a game—until it's no longer a game. Get her!"

The crowd jumped up to block Jo's path. Oh, great, hundreds against one! Now what? But then it hit her—she still had a weapon! She quickly yanked the Tin Woodman's ax from her harness and spun around like a whirlwind. With each twirl, she sent the teens crashing down like dominos, toppling them to the floor as she continued her descent.

With her eyes fixated on the characters, she failed to notice two Wordmen creeping up on her from either side. Before she could react, they each grabbed her by the arm. Panic surged through her as she thrashed against their hold, desperate to break free.

"Let. Me. Go!" she screamed. The Wordmen tightened their grip, hoisting her off her feet as she flailed wildly, kicking at the air in a futile attempt to escape. Her heart sank, terror flooding her veins as she faced the chilling prospect of being brought face-to-face with Silas.

Out of nowhere, an arrow with a trailing rope whizzed through the air just above her head. It struck a thick tent pole, sinking deep into the wood. Then a very welcomed voice called out to her. "Hey! New Girl!"

Still struggling against the grip of the Wordmen, Jo glanced back as Drew zip-lined toward her, using his goggles as a pulley over the rope. Are you serious? Drew collided with her from behind, wrapped his arm around her waist, and lifted her up and away from the Wordmen.

As their momentum slowed over the stage, Drew leaned in close, his breath warm against her ear. "I'm going to let go. Ready?"

Jo nodded. "Ready."

They landed with a thud on the wooden stage. Drew jumped up first and offered Jo his hand. As she took it, those pesky butterflies fluttered around her belly while he helped her up. "You okay?" he asked.

"Yeah. Thanks for saving me. Again," she replied.

"It's kinda become our thing, hasn't it?" he said with a grin. Before she could respond, Drew pulled another arrow from his quiver.

"Incoming!"

The Wordmen they had just thwarted were charging toward them. "Go free the characters," Drew urged. "I'll cover you!"

Jo couldn't help but smile at his courage to defend her. "Robin, your bravery inspires me."

Drew pulled his shoulders back, obviously pleased with her response. "Thank you, m'lady. Now, quickly, go!"

As Jo sprinted toward the characters, Drew nocked the arrow onto his bowstring and confronted the fast-approaching Wordmen. "Get thee gone, straightway, or, by all the saints in heaven, I'll baste thy hides right merrily." Drew fired an arrow at their feet, causing them to halt. "The next shaft I send will go clean through that paper heart of yours before a curtal friar can say grace over a roast goose."

Jo rushed to the characters and immediately chopped through the rope with her axe to free them. "Go! Run and hide. You're all in terrible danger!"

Jo shot a look at Silas's obedient audience. Teens were descending from the bleachers, surging across the floor toward the stage. Hundreds of them acting like robots on a mission. When she glanced back at the characters, they remained frozen in place—even Dorothy, who held Toto against her chest. "Please! Go! He wants to destroy you." She looked right into Dorothy's eyes. "Please?"

"You need us, Jo. Each of us has something special to offer.

Just believe in us!" Dorothy said.

Just then, a shadow swept over Jo, and she saw the Reluctant Dragon swooping toward the crowd. Startled, the teens halted in their tracks. Jake pumped a fist, and he and Noah took advantage of the gap in the crowd and ran up the stairs to the stage. A Wordman lunged to block them, but Noah swung Aladdin's lamp, knocking him out cold.

The militant audience surged forward again, but the Dragon made another pass, forcing them to retreat.

Jake rushed across the stage toward the seven dwarfs standing guard over Snow White. "Which one of you wants the pickaxe?" They all raised their tiny hands. As he handed the pickaxe to one of them, he quipped, "Let me guess … you're Sneezy?" The Dwarf shook his head. "Doc? Sleepy? Happy? Bashful? Grumpy?" With each guess, the dwarf shook his head, frustration mounting. "Who am I missing?"

From behind, someone tapped him on the shoulder. "Dopey!"

Jake spun around to find Cleet's glowing yellow eyes peering at him from behind his goggles.

In an instant, Cleet unleashed a savage punch to Jake's nose, sending him crashing to the ground. Cleet planted his foot on Jake's chest, sneering. "You should have joined us, Nerd. Now I'm gonna finish you off." He raised his boot above Jake's face, then suddenly was knocked out cold. Jake looked up, relieved to see the dwarf standing protectively over him, gripping the pickaxe tightly.

Under the glaring spotlight at center stage, Silas stood surrounded by his loyal Wordmen. He watched with some satisfaction as two Wordmen carried Pinocchio toward the fiery pit.

Sara started to run toward him, but a Wordman caught her and held her tight. "Lie, Pinocchio!" she yelled in desperation. "Lie!"

Pinocchio, still struggling against his captors, turned towards Sara's voice. "I never lie!" he declared, though his nose told a different tale, shooting out from his face like a wooden shaft that poked the eye of one of the Wordmen. The Wordman howled in pain and released his grip on Pinocchio, who quickly turned his head the other way and slammed his wooden nose against the other Wordman's face. As the Wordman staggered back, Pinocchio dropped to the floor and rolled away from the edge of the fiery pit.

Sara cheered at his escape, then drove her elbow into the Wordman's gut and stomped hard on his foot. As he doubled over in pain, Sara took off.

While the dragon flew low to hold the militant audience at bay, Drew and Robin Hood stood back-to-back on the edge of the stage, fending off the attacks of the Wordmen. Drew quickly pulled an arrow from the quiver and passed it to Robin as a Wordman advanced toward them. "On your east," Drew shouted. Together, they moved in a half circle, and Robin fired off an arrow at their adversary.

"South," Drew yelled as he passed Robin another arrow. The

pair spun around, and Robin once again proved his reputation as an excellent archer.

Meanwhile, Ezra stood in the shadows of the stage and studied his boss's face. Silas was seething with anger. Ezra knew those kids would soon learn what retribution looked like.

Silas growled in frustration at the incompetence of his Wordmen failing to stop this unexpected turn of events. His gaze narrowed as he sought the source of his deep irritation. Jo March had pushed him too far. There were only two ways to deal with a worthy adversary. She had to join his cause—or die.

As they neared the edge of the fiery pit, Hansel and Gretel recoiled from the Wordman bearing down on them. Feeling the heat at their back, the pair stopped to plead for mercy. But the Wordman merely sneered at their terror and stepped closer. The kids' eyes widened in fear as the Wordman reached out to shove them into the flames, but Noah interrupted, striking the back of his head with Aladdin's lamp. Stumbling from the impact, the Wordman was met with a mighty push from Gretel, sending him screaming into the fire pit. Noah grinned and held up his palm for a high-five, but Gretel's lingered elsewhere. "Hey. Don't leave me hanging," he chuckled.

"Noah! Watch out!" Jo shouted. Turning to her, Noah saw Jo pointing at a Wordman barreling toward him. With his hand still raised for a high-five, he yelled, "Expecto Patronum!"

The Wordman charged ahead, arms outstretched, to topple Noah backward into the fiery pit. Just then, a cascade of golden hair fell right beside him. Noah looked up to see Rapunzel perched in the tent's rigging. He called out to Jo, "Catch!" Tossing her Aladdin's lamp, he grabbed hold of Rapunzel's hair and swung out of the way just as the Wordman lunged. Missing his target, the Wordman shrieked as he plummeted into the flames below.

Jo, holding Aladdin's lamp, looked at the scenes all around her. There were teens who had managed to breach the Dragon's effort to keep them off the stage. Drew and Robin Hood were still valiantly trying to fend off the Wordmen and keep them away from the characters, but she knew they couldn't hold on forever.

"Could you please return my lamp to me?"

She looked down at Aladdin's outstretched hand. A thief … that's what we need right now.

"I'll trade you your lamp for a favor." She leaned closer to Aladdin and gave him her terms.

Aladdin flashed a rakish grin at her. "Your wish is my command. Yet, I must confess, my finest deeds are done beneath the veil of night."

As Aladdin took off, Jo glanced over at Silas standing in the bright spotlight surrounding him and his Wordmen. Veil of night … that's it!

Jo sprinted across the stage to Robin and Drew. "I need you to take out that spotlight over Silas!"

"At your service, my fair lady," Robin replied with a grin.

In one swift motion, he fired off an arrow, which shattered the spotlight, plunging Silas and his Wordmen into darkness.

Silas's booming voice cut through the chaos of the Big Top. "Get the lights back on! Now!"

Utility lights blinked on in moments, revealing the fury on the face of the man who embodied all the evil thoughts of his maker. A wave of fear washed over her.

"No mercy. No grace," Silas shouted. "Kill anyone who is not part of my Wehrmacht!"

Jo knew she was staring into the face of pure evil when Silas made his hateful declaration. Her hope for saving her beloved characters shattered into a million pieces. There was no doubt that Silas would exterminate her literary heroes, and she feared for the safety of herself and her friends. *And it's all my fault. Dorothy and the others shouldn't be here. Polly, Sara, Drew, Noah, and Jake! I'm so sorry. I'm sorry I put everyone in danger!*

Obeying the orders of their commander, the Wordmen sprang into action and seized Polly. One Wordman bound her wrists with a rope, while the other fashioned what appeared to be a noose.

As Polly struggled against her captors, Noah and Snow White were being dragged on their backs across the stage toward the pit and certain death. The dwarfs raced after Snow White, but the teenage soldiers blocked their path, encircling them with malevolent grins.

Jo's heart raced, feeling as if it might burst from her chest. In her panic, she desperately searched for anyone or anything that could stop Silas and his madness.

"May I have my lamp back?" Aladdin's voice came through the din.

She turned to see him with his fist raised, and a wave of gratitude nearly made her collapse. Without hesitation, she handed him the lamp.

Stepping to center stage where Silas would surely notice her, she shouted above the cacophony of battle. "Silas!"

She waited until the man himself turned to look at her with a sneer curling on his lips. Then, raising the small remote with the big red button, Jo watched as his sneer vanished, replaced by a fierce anger that was so palpable, she could almost feel it in the air.

"Don't do it!" Silas roared at her.

Jo pressed the red button. Immediately, the goggles flicked off, and the yellow eyes vanished. The teens looked confused and disoriented. No longer under Silas's control, they turned to each other and wondered what had just happened.

Filled with immense relief, Jo hollered to the White Rose book club to help each other out. Polly and Noah were safe now. The dwarfs had rescued Snow White. Drew and the others gathered together, and Jo was walking to join them when Silas's voice rang out.

"Jo March! This isn't over!"

Jo whirled around to find Silas, his face twisted with rage as he held Dorothy dangerously close to the fiery pit. Dorothy, clutching Toto to her chest, looked terrified.

"Don't! Please! I'm begging you to spare her!" Jo shouted, sprinting toward Silas and Dorothy.

"Do you have any idea how much time and money you have cost me, Miss March? Years of planning for this event have been ruined by your childish obsession to protect your precious literary characters!"

Jo saw the fear on Dorothy's face and the hundreds of teens observing their tense exchange. She couldn't allow Dorothy to be consumed by the flames. If that were to happen, she would never forgive herself.

"Take me instead," Jo said.

"Jo! What are you doing?" Dorothy cried.

"No, Jo, don't do it," Polly called out.

But Jo ignored them and started toward Silas.

"Like you said, I'm the cause of all your trouble. You know I won't stay silent about what you're planning. I'll expose you for the evil that you are."

"Fine! Trade accepted." Once Silas had a grip on Jo, he released Dorothy and Toto, who quickly joined the Scarecrow and her other companions.

Jo turned to Dorothy. "I just want you to know that meeting you and spending time together has been a dream of mine."

"Blah, blah, blah!" Silas sneered. "Run back to Oz, little Dorothy, before I change my mind. And as for you, Jo March, time for you to meet your demise."

"It doesn't matter what you say or do," she said in an unwavering voice. "Good will always triumph over evil."

Silas, a dark glimmer in his eyes, sneered at her defiant words. "I believe we're about to rewrite that narrative, don't you?" he taunted. "I could use you in my army. You have 'general' written all over you. Are you ready to pledge your loyalty to me and become one of my SS warriors? If so, I might just spare your life."

Jo swallowed hard, a flicker of doubt crossing her face. For a moment, she pondered Silas's sinister proposition. Then, gathering her resolve, she spoke with fierce determination. "I would rather die."

An evil grin spread across Silas's face, his eyes gleaming with malevolence. Without hesitation, he pushed Jo forcefully.

She let out a piercing scream as she tumbled backward, her reflexes kicking in just in time for her to grab hold of Silas's arm. In a desperate attempt to save herself, she exerted every ounce of strength, pulling him over the edge with her. Silas dangled precariously by his fingertips, his right hand barely clinging onto the plank. Jo, her hands gripping tightly around his leg, heard the strain in his voice as he snarled, "Let go, you little fool!"

Ezra stood by, watching Silas dangle over the fiery pit, and envisioned his own future unfolding. With the boss out of the picture, he would finally hold the power. He glanced down at the pouch containing the Powder of Life he had kept safe. Then, he took one last look at the man who had dictated his every action and slipped away.

As her grip on Silas's leg slowly slipped, Jo's terrified gaze darted downwards to the inferno below. Its deep red, almost black hue sent fiery flames shooting upward, threatening to engulf her shoes. However, in that perilous moment, a flicker of determination sparked within her.

"Oh," she uttered, her expression transforming into one of steadfast resolve as she locked eyes with Silas. Straining against the force of gravity, Jo spoke through gritted teeth, "I told you good always wins."

Silas felt his grip faltering, his fingers losing their tenuous hold on the plank. Hearing a tapping sound growing louder with each passing second, he glanced frantically downward, only to be met with a chilling realization.

"Take me home to my parents," the tapping echoed relentlessly. "Take me home to my parents." Silas's heart sank as the truth dawned on him. It was those blasted shoes that had betrayed him. With a final, desperate struggle to maintain his grasp, Silas's hand slipped off the edge of the plank, condemning him to the same fate he had intended for Jo.

Chapter 24
No Place Like Home

Jo's eyes opened slowly; her vision was hazy as she tried to make out the blurry shapes around her. The first thing that came into focus was Nimble, perched on her chest, his whiskers twitching furiously, intently studying her. A disembodied voice filled the room, calling out her name.

"Jo? Honey?" the voice said, a mix of concern and relief. "Eve?! Is she awake?!" Another voice chimed in, sounding hurried. As Jo pulled her arms free of a blanket, Nimble scampered down to her legs while she struggled to sit up. Adam rushed over and crouched beside her.

Confused, Jo looked into the relieved expressions on her parents' faces.

She frowned, trying to make sense of what was happening.

"Welcome back, munchkin," Adam said affectionately.

Jo glanced around, still trying to comprehend the situation. "Back? Where?" She put a tentative hand on her throbbing head.

"We didn't exactly make our two-month goal ... you smacked your head pretty good," Adam explained.

Evelyn chimed in; her tone was reassuring. "But no stitches. Just an enormous lump. Possible concussion though ..."

As Jo's memories began to resurface, she slowly started to piece together the events that had unfolded. "I remember all the characters running loose in the city," she started, her voice growing more animated. "Well, they weren't inanimate anymore because of the Powder of Life, and my friends and I were with Dorothy and Robin Hood and Aladdin and so many others, and then Silas took them..."

Evelyn exchanged a glance with Adam; their surprise was obvious. Jo's words spilled out faster as memories rushed back to her. "... and all I could think about was how to save all the characters from the fire ... but then I remembered how Dorothy got home, and I clicked my heels as I fell ..."

Her mom and dad exchanged knowing looks, a mix of understanding and amusement.

"It was just a dream, Jo," Evelyn said gently, her tone reassuring. "Just a jumble of stories from all those books you've read over the years."

Jo shook her head, desperation creeping into her voice. "But it felt so real! I could swear it actually happened!"

Adam, the ever-wise one, added, "We often dream in our

waking moments and walk in our sleep."

As Jo thought about it, she looked towards the large door of the enchanted room. To her surprise, the wax characters were back where they belonged. She was both confused and immensely relieved at the same time.

"A dream?" she whispered, trying to make sense of it all. Then another realization struck her. "Wait ... I never experienced a dizzy spell. Not once."

Adam grinned, leaning towards her. "You see, munchkin? It couldn't have been anything more than a vivid dream, though it's not surprising. It's pure Literary Chaos down here!"

Jo couldn't help but feel a pang of disappointment. She truly believed that she had embarked on an incredible adventure. Evelyn placed a comforting hand on Jo's arm. Her voice was gentle but firm. "What's real, Jo, is that you're going to be fine. And we love you very much."

Jo looked at the faces of her mom and dad. She knew they loved her—no matter what. "I know you do. Even if you decide to ... not stay married."

Her dad glanced at her mom, who offered a tiny smile. Then he took Jo's hand. "Listen, munchkin. Your mom and I have let the pressures from outside our family influence how we've been behaving toward each other."

"What does that mean?" Jo asked.

"It means you gave us quite a scare. We thought our decision made you run away from home. When I figured out you were gone, I immediately called your mom. She's the only one in the world who loves you as much as I do—who worries about you—who shares all my memories of you. She's the one who figured out that you would never run away without Nimble, who was still in your room."

"What your dad is trying to say, Jo, is that we have realized that we need to ignore all the noise of the world and remember why we became a family in the first place," her mom said.

"So that means you won't be staying with your friend Shelly?" Jo asked.

Her mom smiled. "Yes, that's what it means."

Adam's eyes softened as he looked at his daughter. "You may have given us quite a scare, but you also reminded us of what truly matters. We want this to work—all of us together. We just need to do the work to make that happen."

The warm glow of happiness enveloped Jo. "Setting out on an adventure is thrilling, but coming home … there's no place like it."

She put her hand out, and Nimble climbed right into it. After pushing aside the blanket over her legs, she tentatively stood up. Her parents hovered close by. "I'm okay," Jo said, "really."

Instead of heading up the stairs, Jo made her way to the enchanted room and stopped at the threshold. Strange. The wolf isn't here. Then, she took in the breathtaking sight of all her beloved characters. Her gaze stopped on Dorothy, and she marveled once again at the magnificent detail of the character. The bonnet, the dress, the braids, the … wait … no shoes. Jo swung her eyes downward and gasped in surprise. Dorothy wasn't wearing her silver shoes—because Jo was.

Chapter 25
Friendship Is Not Words but Meanings

ONE WEEK LATER

Jo made her way into the cafeteria, where lunch was already underway. She paused at the entrance and surveyed the crowded room. There was the usual buzz of conversations between the kids eating lunch. The jocks were congregated around their table while cheerleaders were sharing videos from phones and laughing. Everything seemed pleasantly normal to Jo. She spotted Polly, Sara, Jake, Noah, and even Drew sitting at their usual lunch table. As she made her way across the room, she noticed Miss Windsor tracking her. Jo offered a smile, and in return, Miss Windsor pointed two fingers at her own eyes, then pointed at Jo, which made it clear. I'm watching you. As Jo passed the table with Rose, Carrie, and the rest of the cheer squad, Rose totally ignored her, but Carrie caught her eye and gave a slight nod. Just then, Polly called her name and motioned for her to join the book club. As she approached, they all greeted her enthusiastically.

"When you weren't here this morning, I didn't think you'd be back today," Polly said.

"I had to get a release from the doctor before I could return to school," Jo said. "I'm so glad to be back. I was going stir-crazy at home."

Jake piped up, "Your mom told us about your nasty concussion when we stopped by to check on you."

"It was so nice of you guys to do that," Jo said. "I'm sorry I was asleep. My mom should have woken me up."

"We were dying to talk to you," Polly said, "but we understood completely when your mom told us you needed your rest. She was really nice and assured us you were going to be fine."

"If it makes you feel any better, Jo, I broke my nose the other weekend, but now I'm fine too," Jake said.

"You mean from being punched in the face by that Neanderthal Cleet?"

Jake leaned toward her. "How do you know that?"

Jo shrugged, sheepish. "This is going to sound nuts, but I had this impossible, crazy … I guess you'd call it a dream … about the Big Top Domain, and you were all in it."

Jo watched the kids exchange knowing glances. "See? You

already think I'm bonkers again."

"Not true. Go on," Drew urged. "Really. We want to hear about it."

Jo sighed. "Okay. But I'm not sure I can even begin to explain how real it all seemed."

Jake looked past Jo. "Speak of the devil …"

Jo turned to see Cleet Ambrose, wearing sunglasses and carrying his lunch tray, walking toward their table. "Uh oh."

"It's okay, Jo," Jake said, keeping his eyes on Cleet.

Cleet stopped at the table. "Here." He took two Twinkies from his tray and put them down in front of Jake with a smile.

Jake smiled back. "Thanks, Cleet."

Cleet nodded. "Welcome."

Jo was astonished as she watched him walk away. "I wouldn't eat that if I were you."

She turned back to see Jake frozen mid-air, a Twinkie just inches from his mouth. He looked at her as she continued, "I mean, did you guys make up? Did he apologize for punching you? Have I been gone long enough for Cleet to have a personality transplant?"

"Nope, but I won't say no to a free Twinkie." Jake took a big bite.

"I think Cleet saw the error of his mean ways and has changed for the better," Polly said. "It's not impossible."

Drew rapped his knuckles on the table. "So enough about Cleet and Twinkies. Let's get back to your dream."

"Like the skeleton in the gibbet," Noah blurted out.

Jo's eyes grew wide with surprise. "What did you just say?"

"The glowing Powder of Life," Sara said.

"The journal," Jake said.

"There was some seriously spooky stuff down there, Jo," Polly said. "Once we went through the wardrobe, we were all surprised."

At first, Jo was speechless. "I don't understand how it's possible for you to know any of that."

"But it's all true, right?" Jake said.

Jo nodded. "Yes."

"Just like it's true that Aladdin, Dorothy, Scarecrow, Robin Hood, and many others were scattered around the city, and we all split up to find them," Noah said.

"Then at the Big Top Domain when we were wearing the creepy goggleth and reality got all thcrewed up," Sara said.

Jo looked stunned. "I thought I was going crazy, and now you're telling me my dream, with all of you in it, was real?"

"We've had the last week to talk about it," Drew said. "Little details started spilling out, then big details. We've been going nuts waiting to hear from you. And now we know. We all had the same shared real experience."

"Well, except for the goggles," Polly added. "Because you had the good sense not to put them on. You saved the characters and all of us. A real hero, Jo."

"Honestly, if it weren't for my Meniere's disease, I would have been pulled into Silas's trap just like everyone else," Jo admitted.

Jake looked solemn. "Made me feel like I was invincible. I felt so … powerful. Strong. I wanted to keep feeling that way."

Sara nodded. "I wathn't me. I felt ten feet tall and didn't recognize the things I wath thaying and doing. I liked it but didn't like it at the thame time."

"Same for me when I had the goggles on," Polly said. "It's hard to explain the overwhelming desire to stay in that world."

"Totally freaky experience," Noah said. "Not my usual Oculus vibe at all."

"It's true. You did feel invincible somehow," Drew said. "Like nothing could touch you. But somehow, you knew you should resist."

"I still think about how it felt," Noah admitted.

"Me too," Jake said. "Sometimes I can almost feel like that

again. Almost."

The other kids nodded. Jo was speechless.

"How is any of this even possible?" Jo asked.

"No idea," Noah said. "We've been wracking our brains trying to come up with a logical explanation."

"I even threw out the idea of Body Transfer Illusion as a possibility, but that doesn't fit either," Jake said. "It's like we were in the upside-down world from Stranger Things."

Jo took a moment to let it sink in. "It really happened. The characters … they were there. I'm not crazy."

"You were so brave, Jo, when you saved Dorothy and Silas tried to throw you into the fire pit," Noah said.

"Then you disappeared, and we didn't know what happened to you," Polly said. "With all the evil … I imagined all kinds of bad things. Not my usual go-to."

"You guys were worried about me?" Jo asked.

Drew looked at Jo with a soft smile; his voice filled with affection. "Let's just say our hearts fell when you did."

Touched by his words, Jo blushed as she remembered a quote: "A lady's imagination is very rapid; it jumps from admiration to love, from love to matrimony in a moment." Jo was glad Drew couldn't read her mind. She started to thank him, but Noah interrupted her.

"We've all been wondering, and I'm almost afraid to ask, but do you know what happened to all the characters?" Noah asked.

Jo nodded. "They're safely back in the enchanted room where I first found them."

The kids breathed a collective sigh of relief.

"Well, all of them except for the Wolf," Jo said. "To be honest, I'm happy that the wolf is gone."

"What's going to happen to them now?" Drew asked.

"Ideally, they need to go to a place where the public can appreciate them. All the amazing craftsmanship and artistry," Jo said. "But my dad is concerned the backstory of who created them might be a problem. He plans to reach out to the Boston Public Library first to see if they would be interested. Maybe it will inspire more kids to read."

"That's awesome," Polly said. "It means we can visit them anytime."

Jo smiled. "Even if they stayed at my house, you're more than welcome to see them anytime."

Noah piped up. "No offense, Jo, but that basement of yours is beyond creepy."

Jake nodded and even shuddered a bit, but then he looked at Jo. "Talking about creepy. Did you see what happened to Silas?"

"A couple of snippets online about a fire," Jo said. "But my mom and dad tried to limit my screen time because of the concussion."

Noah pushed a newspaper across the table toward Jo. "We still get the paper at my house. I saved it for you." On the front page was a picture of what was left of the Big Top Domain.

Jo read the headline: "Chaos at the Big Top." She continued to read. "All that remains of the Big Top Domain is a pile of ashes. The fire broke out after midnight, well after hundreds of teens had attended the traveling techno carnival. Authorities are still trying to piece together what Silas Schutzstaffel was attempting to achieve with his high-tech spectacle but have not been able to locate him for an interview."

Sara shuddered, disgust evident in her tone. "Whatever he wath trying to achieve, we know it wathn't good. The whole thing ith awful ... and ethpethally groth that the only body they found in the atheth had been dead for decadeth."

"Another mystery. How is that even possible?" Jake asked.

"I think I might have the explanation," Jo said.

"We're all ears," Noah said.

"Even though my parents couldn't quite wrap their heads around my dream—that apparently wasn't a dream—they still wanted an explanation for the characters and the skeleton in our secret basement. My dad went into research mode. He started by investigating the previous owners of our home. One of which was Samuel Sawyer."

"Is that the guy who created the characters and the Powder of Life?" Noah asked.

"Yes." Jo paused for dramatic effect and revealed the shocking truth. "But the skeleton in our basement wasn't Samuel Sawyer. There is still some testing to do, but after looking at dental records and authenticating the Nazi uniform, the initial evidence points to someone named Karl Romberg, a German officer in Hitler's army. He was the physician in charge of the children that were considered rejects, and he had them put to death."

They were dumbfounded, unable to comprehend the magnitude of this revelation. Polly finally found her words, quietly expressing her disbelief: "Maybe we would have been some of the rejects."

The kids all considered her statement and nodded. "Entirely possible," Jake said. "But back to Silas. I still don't understand …"

"I have a theory about that. Silas was dead—and then he wasn't," Jo said. "Thanks to the Powder of Life."

"Let me get this straight. Samuel, aka Karl Romberg, finds a corpse, creates the Powder of Life, then brings him back from the dead?"

Jo nodded. "I believe had Karl survived, it would have been

Silas in that gibbet in my basement. In some twisted way, he wanted Silas to take on his sins so he could be innocent. He wanted the corpse to pay for all the evil he did to the children under his care."

"I guess he missed the memo that Jesus takes away sins, not some corpse," Noah said.

"What do you suppose happened to the Powder of Life?" Polly asked.

"I hope it's a smoldering pile of ash in the remnants of the Big Top," Jo said.

Before the kids could respond, someone behind her called her name. She turned around as Carrie approached their table like a girl on a mission.

"Hey, Jo. Got a second?"

Jo shrugged. "Sure. What's up?"

"I heard you had a concussion or something."

Jo nodded. "Yeah, I did. I'm better now."

"Good." Carrie looked uncomfortable. "Listen, I owe you an apology for being so crappy to you on your first day of school."

"It's okay," Jo said.

Carrie shook her head. "No. It's not. We were so mean to you. We didn't even know you and were mean. And then your mouse almost died, and all we cared about was getting you in trouble with Miss Windsor. It's been bugging me ever since, and then when I heard you'd gotten hurt, I felt even more terrible."

"Let's forget it ever happened," Jo said.

Carrie finally smiled. "Thanks, Jo. I'm sure I wouldn't be as forgiving if someone did all that to me. What's your secret?"

Jo took a second to think about it, then said, "My secret is books. The literary classics. When you read a great story, you go on a journey with characters who have thoughts, feelings, and fears just like we do. When they work through stuff like good versus evil, love, and loss, and reach their goals, it makes the reader feel we can do the same."

"So that's why you love books."

"That's definitely part of it. What I love most about the classics is their sense of wonder and enchantment. A safe place to escape and be transported by my imagination to magical worlds where anything is possible. And I do mean anything!"

"Bookmarks are for quitters."

Jo smiled broadly. "If you want, I can put a list together of my faves."

"I'd like that. Thanks, Jo." Carrie turned and made her way back to the table with the cheerleaders.

"See? There's good in everyone," Polly said.

Jo turned and let her gaze drift over the kids in the cafeteria. First, Cleet's odd behavior, and now Carrie. While she welcomed their change of heart, it still felt puzzling. Perhaps she was reading too much into it; after all, people could change. She turned back to her friends. "So, I'll bet the Big Top was the topic of conversation at school after what happened."

Drew shook his head. "Strangely no. You'd think after the intense experience everyone had, they'd still be talking about it, but nope. It's almost like it never happened at all."

"That is strange," Jo agreed. "We saved hundreds of kids at the Big Top from Silas—and they'll never know it."

"Maybe we should tell them. I'm sure they'd appreciate it," Polly said.

"Ha! Bad idea. We'd go from being the book club nerds to the crazy book club nerds," Jake said. "Besides, no one would believe it. We barely believe it!"

"We'd never be able to explain it," Noah said. "It's too impossible."

Jo shook her head. "Not impossible. In the middle of all the chaos, all the literary chaos, there was one steady force that united us on our mission. We went to the Big Top to save the characters we love and ended up saving the kids from something seriously dark and evil. All thanks to the incredible books with characters that leap off the page. They come alive in our world, make us fall in love with them, and we think about them long after the author writes 'the end.'"

"I love a good ending," Polly said.

"Me too," Jo said. Out of the corner of her eye, she noticed Cleet walk up to Carrie, holding up a pair of goggles by the strap. She smiled at him before quickly grabbing the goggles and stuffing them into her backpack.

Jo looked at the faces of her new friends with a severe sense of foreboding. "Suddenly, I get the feeling that there is still a plot twist in store for our happy ending."

EPILOGUE
The Past Is Not Dead

Beneath the glow of a full moon, the once serene cemetery stirred with an unusual activity. A hooded, shadowy figure, dressed in black from head to toe, toiled away, vigorously digging up a grave in the dead of night. The shovel struck the casket with a resounding thud, and the digger grunted with satisfaction. Pausing briefly, the digger knelt and deftly undid the latch on the casket, revealing its morbid contents.

Stretching out on a luxurious bed of white silk lay the lifeless body of a man in his prime who had only recently departed this world.

The digger pushed the hood off his head, and the moon caught his pleased expression. "Remarkable condition," Ezra murmured approvingly.

Producing the passport pouch from around his neck, he carefully opened it, pinched a small amount between his thumb and index finger, and blew the Powder of Life onto the face of the deceased. Ezra waited and watched, confident things would go his way.

With a sudden blink, the man's yellow eyes flickered open.

"Rise," Ezra declared authoritatively.

Extending his hand, Ezra offered his help, which the resurrected man gratefully accepted. As they emerged from the confines of the grave, the man surveyed his surroundings.

"You shall join the others," Ezra instructed, gesturing towards a gathering of animated corpses nearby. Ezra watched the walking-dead corpse move with a stiff gait toward his peers.

Ezra brushed the dirt off his trousers with his hands and then made his way toward a shadowy figure who stood motionless under a withered, spindly tree. The figure's breathing reached his ears before he caught sight of its piercing yellow eyes and sharp teeth.

"What now, boss?" Ezra asked reluctantly.

The Wolf, dressed in his familiar nightgown, stepped aside to reveal Cleet Ambrose, who sported his football jersey and sunglasses. A predatory look crossed Cleet's face as he furrowed his brow.

"You cannot make a revolution with silk gloves."

"Yeah, they wouldn't go well with the wolf's nightie," Ezra quipped, unable to resist a joke.

Cleet glanced at the Wolf and gave him a subtle nod that instantly transformed the Wolf's expression into a broad grin, revealing his sharp, white teeth.

"Those are some big teeth you've got," Ezra remarked nervously.

Cleet removed his sunglasses, exposing his striking yellow eyes. "Better to eat you with." And the Wolf lunged at Ezra.

Quotes from Literary Chaos

Frankenstein by **Mary Shelley**

Page 54   "You can't stay in your corner of the forest waiting for others to come to you. You have to go to them sometimes."

Winnie the Pooh by **A.A. Milne**

Page 61   "Make sure everything you do is so completely crazy, it's unbelievable."

Matilda, by **Roald Dahl**

Page 62   "I don't want to ruin an apology with an excuse."

Benjamin Franklin

Page 67   "For there to be betrayal, there would have to have been trust."

The Hunger Games by **Suzanne Collins**

Page 74   "Once upon a midnight dreary, while I pondered, weak and weary, over many a quaint and curious volume of forgotten lore – while I nodded, nearly napping, suddenly there came a tapping, as if someone gently rapping…"

The Raven by **Edgar Allan Poe**

Page 77   "There is nothing in the world so irresistible contagious as laughter and good humor."

Page 123   "A lady's imagination is very rapid; it jumps from admiration to love, from love to matrimony in a moment."

Pride and Prejudice by **Jane Austen**

Page 130   "You cannot make a revolution with silk gloves."

Joseph Stalin

Acknowledgments

To Alexandra Ott for her invaluable editorial acumen and to Stefano
Buro for his imaginative and unique cover art.

Our heartfelt thanks and appreciation for the authors of the classics –

some written decades ago – some written centuries ago,

but whose themes are still relevant today.

Their masterful storytelling and limitless imagination

Continue to inspire storytellers – like us.

About The Authors

Michael Landon Jr., son of legendary television and film icon Michael Landon, has built an impressive career spanning over three decades. After studying at USC and the American Film Institute, he achieved his breakthrough with "Love Comes Softly," which became Hallmark Channel's highest-rated film and generated over 2 million DVD sales. Its sequel, "Love's Enduring Promise," surpassed these records.

As a writer, director, and producer, Landon has created over two dozen films, including theatrical releases like "The Velveteen Rabbit" and socially impactful projects such as "Jamaa" for World Vision. Landon's credits include "When Calls the Heart," a movie he wrote, directed, and produced featuring talented stars like Maggie Grace, Stephen Amell, Jean Smart, and Lori Loughlin. It became the backdoor pilot for the beloved television series, now in its 12th season, making it the longest-running series in Hallmark Channel history. He continues to executive produce both this series and its spin-off, "When Hope Calls" for GAF.

Currently, Landon is developing the TV series "Home to Harmony" and a documentary on race reconciliation titled "The Dream King." In addition to his work in television and film, Landon has co-authored four published novels. His greatest joy is his wife, Sharee, and their three children.

Cindy Kelley has had a writing partnership with Landon that spans over two decades. Together they have seven screenwriting credits and besides their latest book, Literary Chaos, they have written three previous novels: The Silent Gift, Traces of Mercy, and Finding Mercy. Cindy lives in Southern Arizona with her husband Jim, and has three grown children and six grandchildren.